Slocum _____s
cheek _____w
so _____ to
Slocum's shoulder, but took two hard hits under his eyes
that staggered him.

"You're going to learn some manners this evening,"
Slocum said, dodging a wild haymaker and nailing in two
more quick fists to Bixby's head.

"About what?"

"About who you call a bitch."

"IIa, her—"

Slocum's fist pounded his nose, and Bixby ducked back,
slinging blood. "I'll call that bitch a bitch—"

"Not while I'm around." Filled with a newfound fury,
Slocum moved in, and in five punches had the big man
sprawled on his back. He stood over him ready for any attempt by him to get up.

DON'T MISS THESE
ALL-ACTION WESTERN SERIES
FROM THE BERKLEY PUBLISHING GROUP

THE GUNSMITH *by J. R. Roberts*

Clint Adams was a legend among lawmen, outlaws, and ladies. They called him . . . the Gunsmith.

LONGARM *by Tabor Evans*

The popular long-running series about Deputy U.S. Marshal Long—his life, his loves, his fight for justice.

SLOCUM *by Jake Logan*

Today's longest-running action Western. John Slocum rides a deadly trail of hot blood and cold steel.

BUSHWHACKERS *by B. J. Lanagan*

An action-packed series by the creators of Longarm! The rousing adventures of the most brutal gang of cutthroats ever assembled—Quantrill's Raiders.

DIAMONDBACK *by Guy Brewer*

Dex Yancey is Diamondback, a Southern gentleman turned con man when his brother cheats him out of the family fortune. Ladies love him. Gamblers hate him. But nobody pulls one over on Dex . . .

WILDGUN *by Jack Hanson*

The blazing adventures of mountain man Will Barlow—from the creators of Longarm!

TEXAS TRACKER *by Tom Calhoun*

Meet J.T. Law: the most relentless—and dangerous—manhunter in all Texas. Where sheriffs and posses fail, he's the best man to bring in the most vicious outlaws—for a price.

JAKE LOGAN

SLOCUM

AND THE BIXBY BATTLE

JOVE BOOKS, NEW YORK

THE BERKLEY PUBLISHING GROUP
Published by the Penguin Group
Penguin Group (USA) Inc.
375 Hudson Street, New York, New York 10014, USA
Penguin Group (Canada), 10 Alcorn Avenue, Toronto, Ontario M4V 3B2, Canada
(a division of Pearson Penguin Canada Inc.)
Penguin Books Ltd., 80 Strand, London WC2R 0RL, England
Penguin Group Ireland, 25 St. Stephen's Green, Dublin 2, Ireland (a division of Penguin Books Ltd.)
Penguin Group (Australia), 250 Camberwell Road, Camberwell, Victoria 3124, Australia
(a division of Pearson Australia Group Pty. Ltd.)
Penguin Books India Pvt. Ltd., 11 Community Centre, Panchsheel Park, New Delhi—110 017, India
Penguin Group (NZ), Cnr. Airborne and Rosedale Roads, Albany, Auckland 1310, New Zealand
(a division of Pearson New Zealand Ltd.)
Penguin Books (South Africa) (Pty.) Ltd., 24 Sturdee Avenue, Rosebank, Johannesburg 2196,
South Africa

Penguin Books Ltd., Registered Offices: 80 Strand, London WC2R 0RL, England

This is a work of fiction. Names, characters, places, and incidents either are the product of the author's imagination or are used fictitiously, and any resemblance to actual persons, living or dead, business establishments, events, or locales is entirely coincidental.

SLOCUM AND THE BIXBY BATTLE

A Jove Book / published by arrangement with the author

PRINTING HISTORY
Jove edition / February 2005

Copyright © 2005 by The Berkley Publishing Group.

ISBN: 0-515-13887-8

JOVE®
Jove Books are published by The Berkley Publishing Group,
a division of Penguin Group (USA) Inc.
375 Hudson Street, New York, New York 10014.
JOVE is a registered trademark of Penguin Group (USA) Inc.
The "J" design is a trademark belonging to Penguin Group (USA) Inc.

PRINTED IN THE UNITED STATES OF AMERICA

10 9 8 7 6 5 4 3 2 1

1

His knuckles rubbing across his beard stubble sounded like a crosscut saw eating up wood. He considered the straight-backed woman sitting in the chair across the sunlit table from him. Perhaps thirty-five years old, her handsome face the rich color of coffee with cream. Dark eyes enclosed by long black lashes that she used for her own purposes of sly flirting. The set of her brown irises carried a hint of the aloofness she even bore underneath the blue dress buttoned to her throat. Small breasts and a willowy figure made her look appealing enough to any man gazing at her under the ancient live oaks filtering the morning's sunbeams.

Wooden wheeled *carretas* powered with dull oxen crept noisily past them. Screaming children skipped and played in the street, not even noticing the two of them. Dead-eyed swampers appeared from the batwing saloon doors to dump their buckets of slop and gray mop water in the gutter. Overhead a chorus of busy birds chattered. Midmorning in the San Antonio square, across from the famous Alamo church's abandoned structure that served years before as the suicide place for the Lone Star's martyrs.

"Does the señora wish for some food?" Tony, the cafe

1

owner, asked. A white apron around his ample waist, he
bowed when he spoke to her.

"Some eggs, frijoles and a few flour tortillas."

"And you, Slocum?"

"You have any beef?" Slocum sat back in the chair and
considered the man. A longtime friend, the restaurant owner was balding in the front and showing signs of his seden-
tary life with a belly behind the apron.

"I could cut some. It is fresh."

"Fine. Roast me some and make the rest like she ordered." He waved his friend off with a laugh. "You can fix
it." With a forefinger to rub an itch beside his mouth, he
turned back to consider his attractive guest at the table.

"So, señora, continue—"

"Call me Amanda."

"Amanda—you say that you want to hire me?"

"Yes, I have checked on your reputation since I arrived
here. They tell me your gun is for hire."

He smiled and shook his head, causing her to stop and
frown with concern written on her olive face.

"You aren't for hire?" Her dark eyes looked troubled. "I
heard them say—"

He put his hand on the table and reached across to gently squeeze hers in reassurance. "I'm not a pistolero, but
you tell me your problems and I'll see if I can help you."

"My grandfather fought for Texas in the revolution. We
are Mexican people, but we are first Texans. Since the war,
people have drifted in here who think we are either Indians
or foreigners. That we have no rights any longer to hold our
land and cattle."

"The law?"

"The law is their man, too."

"If you're bucking the law, señora—I mean, Amanda,
that's a hard business. You really need lawyers, not gunfighters."

"No, I need men to stand up to them." Her lids narrowed

and the anger rose like a boiling pot behind her scathing look at him.

"What's happened so far?" He slipped down in the chair, listening and admiring her full bottom lip, which reminded him of a fresh brown rose petal. He wondered how it would taste.

"They have stolen our cattle, horses and even killed two good men."

"The law has done nothing?" He cocked his head sideways as if this business made little sense to him.

"Nothing." She turned up her palms, showing her long, slender fingers to him.

"Have you spoken to the Texas Rangers?"

"I telegraphed for them."

"What did they say?"

"They never answered me."

He tented his fingertips and touched the end of his nose. "What could I do, if I went down there?"

"You could make them do the right thing."

"Me and what army?" He chuckled in his throat. This woman must think he was some grande hombre.

"My men, the other ranchers—they need a leader. They are not sniveling cowards. They just need someone to tell them what to do next. The sheriff may even listen to you."

"Did your husband send you?" He looked hard at her for his answer.

She shook her head and her sad eyes telegraphed that he had asked the wrong question. "They shot him in the back—three months ago."

"Here's your meal, *mi amigos!*" Tony and a young girl arrived with two large platters heaped with food to set before them: a pile of fresh snowy tortillas freckled with little brown spots from the griddle; a bowl of fresh red salsa and one of green. The girl poured steaming coffee in their mugs and smiled.

"You need anything else?" she asked.

"No," Slocum said. "But we may need help eating all this." He exchanged glances with Amanda and she nodded in agreement.

"You wondered why I am not wearing black?" she asked, busy with her food when they were alone again.

"No."

"Good. I'm glad you understand. Because I do not intend to let Colonel Bixby and his men think that I am hiding behind widowhood."

"I see."

She lowered her voice and leaned toward him to speak in a whisper. "See those two men who just dismounted from their horses down the street?"

Slocum nodded with a hot tortilla in his palm, ready to load with some chunks of blackened steak, scrambled eggs and frijoles. "Who are they?"

"Nichols and Taker."

"Good to know. They follow you up here?"

"Yes. Why else would they be here? They work for Bixby."

Slocum felt certain he could recognize them again. One was short and husky with jet black hair to his collarless shirt; the other was lanky and wore a low-waisted gunbelt to fit his long arms. Number two was also blond-headed and sported a big mustache. Both men had on the common gear of Texas ranch hands—canvas jeans, collarless shirt, vest and high-crowned hat. They'd hooked their bull-hide chaps on their saddle horns after dismounting. Between bites, Slocum watched them go through the batwing doors, acting disinterested in anything else.

Amanda and Slocum worked on their overflowing platters in silence, and the girl came by and refilled their coffee cups. When he had eaten all he could hold, Slocum wiped his mouth on a cloth napkin and then threw it down.

"Enough," he moaned.

"I should quit," she said, amused. Then her face sobered

and she looked at him hard. "I can see dust devils dancing in your head."

He smiled and picked his teeth with a toothpick. "If you can see them you're luckier than I am."

"You never mentioned how much you charged?"

"How much can you afford?"

"Oh—" She looked to the canopy of leaves overhead for help. "Not a whole lot."

"There will be expenses."

"What're they?"

"Twenty dollars, right now."

"Now?"

"Yes," he said, looking down the street toward the saloon entrance where the two men had gone inside.

She drew her purse up in her lap and loosened the drawstrings. She placed two ten-dollar gold pieces on the table. "That enough?"

He nodded, still looking at the hipshot horses tied to the rack, their tails switching flies.

"May I inquire?"

"Those two down there in the cantina won't be back in your country to bother you again."

She made a worried, questioning face at him. "How is that?"

" 'Cause someone's going to convince them that the hill country's bad for their health."

"And?"

He lifted his coffee cup and studied her through the steam vapors, then blew them away before trying to sip it. "That'll be cheap riddance."

"Oh, yes," she said, wiping her mouth carefully on the napkin. "You can hire men here to do that for twenty dollars?"

"Yes. There's men in San Antonio would beat up their own grandmother for a fee."

"Will those two know—"

He shook his head to dismiss her concern. "All they'll know is to get the hell out of this part of Texas and stay away from up there, too."

"You're very resourceful."

"Have to be to stay alive."

"But can I afford you?"

"I think you can." His eyes met hers, and she never glanced aside until they nodded at each other.

"Excuse me," Slocum said and rose. "Don't leave. I need to know more about your operation."

"Certainly, Slocum."

He made his way back to the kitchen and found Tony busy slicing beef off a hindquarter on the butcher block. The big man blinked as if shocked to see him. "Ah, the señora has left already?"

"No, not yet. You know some tough guys that will beat up two hombres and convince them that the hill country is not healthy for them anymore and they must clear out of the country?"

"No problem. Who are they?"

"Two drovers right now down in the Paloma Cantina. One's name is Taker, other's Nichols."

"You want them convinced to ride off?" Tony bent over and with his sharp knife laid open another strip of red meat.

"That's right, and not ever return to the hill country. Here's twenty pesos."

"Whew! For that much, I can get their ears notched, too."

Slocum smiled and nodded that he heard the offer. "Takes that to convince them, do it."

Tony searched around to be certain they were alone. "Where is her husband?"

"Dead."

He gave a broad smile of discovery. "Oh, so you are her new *segundo*?"

"Something like that. Besides, it's time I better shake some of the dust of this place."

Tony nodded that he understood. "Tonight's soon enough to convince them?" He indicated the money on the butcher block with the tip of his long knife.

"Soon enough. *Gracias.*"

"Hey, give her some for me." The man's evil wink was enough, but he hunched his hips toward the butcher block to further demonstrate his meaning. "*Ay, carumba, hombre,* that would be *muy bueno.*"

2

Alfred Bixby, Colonel, CSA, Georgia Third, put his boots on the desktop and leaned back in the swivel chair. A big man, he looked out the open window at the activity in the yard. How long since they silenced the last cannon? Ten years. Only thing he hated was the fact he'd waited so damn long to leave Georgia and come west. All the good places and water in this country was already taken up by the damn Messikins. Hell, his ole pappy got rid of the god-damn Cherokee in Georgia, no reason he couldn't get these brown bastards run out of there and back to Mexico where they belonged.

America was made for the white people, and not for them Roman papal followers either. Protestants made this country. Let them brown bastards go back to Mexico, count their beads and worship idols in their churches. He had his way, he'd ship them all out except those he needed for help. Couldn't get any good black help out here. Be the ruin of this nation—turning all them black savages free. Why, them lazy dogs wouldn't work unless pressed anyway.

"Señor Bixby, would you like some coffee?" The girl in her late teens stood in the doorway holding the silver pot in her hand.

He glanced over and nodded. It was that new girl, Edora. Cute little thing—he wondered if his nephew Cave had screwed her yet. The boy was part billy goat when it came to women. He could hump more pussy than any old tomcat could in one night—he took after his uncle in that way.

"Come over here," Bixby said, waving at the girl to come closer to him when she started to pour his coffee.

"I must be careful. It is very hot."

"Get over here!"

Hesitant at first, she made a step or two closer, until his arm shot out and he drew her hard up against the chair. "How you do like working here?"

"Oh, finc, señor."

"Put that pot on the desk."

She blinked her startled eyes at him, then quickly obeyed. Drawing her fists toward her mouth as he turned her to face him, she tried to speak, but words never came from her mouth.

"You ain't half-bad," he said, holding his hands on her slender waist. She trembled under his fingers. The notion of her fear only aroused him more. He dropped his boots to the floor and twisted around, drawing her between his legs and looking at her budding breasts under the thin blouse.

His hands went up her rib cage and she drew in a frightened breath. Intent now in his purpose, he lifted the material, looking at the exposed brown skin until at last her pink-tinged, pointed nipples stared at him. With a jerk he pulled her closer and closed his mouth on the right one. From her throat came a suppressed half cry of protest. Her hands attempted to pry him from her breast, but that only instilled more desire in his inflamed brain.

"Don't . . . don't," she cried in a soft voice. "Please don't!"

By then he was so fired up, he hoisted her on the desk and pressed her to lie down with one hand while his other hand pushed up her skirt, exposing her shapely legs.

He undid his pants, letting them fall to his boots, and looked down with a smile of pride at his engorged dick that popped out like a sword when he unbuttoned his underwear. She might have been taken by his nephew, but he would show her what it felt like to be screwed by a real man. Ahold of both of her legs, he dragged her to the edge of the desk and laughed aloud as the tears squirted from her eyes.

"You'll like this," he promised her, crowding the desk and poking his rod into her.

"No!" she moaned.

Too late—he was hunching his butt to get his swollen dick inside her narrow walls. It felt so good to be within one so tight. His hands held her hips as he strained to insert more of his shaft into her. Damn, she was tight. She twisted and tried to escape him, but he was going to open her up or die trying. His butt pumping harder and harder, at last the resisting circle gave and he was inside her to the hilt and a loud moan came from her lips.

He gave a cry of victory, intent on satisfying his own needs. With more vigor, he pounded his turgid rod in and out of her, his upper legs bumping hard against the desk edge.

Had she fainted? He didn't give a damn; he kept on going faster and faster, which only made his erection bigger and tighter, the skin so stretched he thought the head of his dick would burst. A great roar came from his throat, his heart pounded in his chest—but still no satisfaction.

"We've got to do something different," he gasped, out of breath. The excruciating pain in his swollen manhood was not going to end. He drew it out of her and took her by the shoulder.

"Get on the floor on your knees," he ordered the pale-faced girl.

Her rheumy eyes looked with a dull expression at him. He half-lifted her off the desk and onto her knees. His hand behind her head, he forced his sore dick in her mouth.

"Suck on it!" He wasn't telling her again.

The feeling of her tongue pressed hard against it struck like lightning to his balls. His seed rose in an explosion and he pressed toward her, filling her mouth and causing her to try to pull away.

Then with a smile he reached down, like his daddy taught him to do to black wenches afterward, and squeezed her nose between his finger and thumb to force her to swallow his load. His pinch caused her throat to react and he felt her down it before he let go.

She bent over in convulsive coughing. He stripped off the slime from his dick, wiped his hand on her blouse and put himself away. Not bad, but not near as good as it would be for him to screw that damn haughty Amanda. He would get her before this was over and make her beg for him to quit.

He gave the girl a good nudge with his boot tips. "Get up, and tonight come to my bed."

Through her wet lashes, she stared at him in disbelief over his words.

"You heard me. Get a bath, clean up and be in my bedroom at dark."

"But I am no *puta* . . ."

"You are now. You're mine. Get out of here!"

Bixby stared out the window. One of the ranch's bitches was coming in heat and the male dogs were having a snarling contest around her. He wondered if those two cowboys, Nichols and Taker, he had sent to follow Amanda were like those horny dogs, and were doing anything besides fucking whores in San Antonio. The night before he'd also sent his nephew Cave and one of his toughest men, Wilson, to check up on her.

Bixby was busy working on his books. If he didn't have all that Yankee gold he had amassed during the war, this range war business would have already drained a damn poor man. He chuckled to himself—he still had a piss pot full of gold left.

"Señor, the sheriff, he is here."

He looked mildly at the short Mexican houseboy and nodded. "Send him in."

"Hey, McKlein, what's new?" He stuck out his hand for the gray-headed lawman in the road-dusted brown suit. "You look like you've been doing some riding."

"Got word that bitch's hired some tough gunslinger in San Anton."

"Who told you that?" Bixby frowned at him.

"I got my sources."

"Here, have some good whiskey. How could one man be a damn threat to us?" He handed the lawman a glass half-full and poured himself one.

"These damn greasers are a damn sight tougher than I ever thought they would be." McKlein scowled at the glass then tossed half of it down.

"Come with me. I intend to end that bitch's indecision about selling to me."

"What've you got?"

"Come along. It's in the shed."

Bixby led him out of the house and to the wagon in the shed. He climbed up and drew back the tarp covering it.

"Where they hell did you get a goddamn cannon?"

"Mountain howitzer. It will make them Messikins shit in their pants and run like hell."

"But you promised me that ranch of hers out of this deal. I want it intact."

Bixby clapped him on the shoulder. "Don't worry. A few rounds from this baby and they will abandon the damn ranch." He laughed aloud over his plan, until McKlein finally joined in.

Damn, Bixby thought, he would like to screw that Debaca woman, but he better use his dick on that house girl for the time being. His time for Amanda would come. He needed to be patient was all. "So, my friend, are we in business or not?"

"We're in business," McKlein agreed.

3

They left the fandango early and hurried up the street. Slocum pulled Amanda by the arm into a dark alcove, then he checked to be certain they were alone before he kissed her. The fire of her breath threatened to melt his freshly shaved upper lip. A deep aroma of flowers saturated his nostrils' lining, and her body molded against him with the same need he felt growing in his pants. The newfound richness of her lips made his head whirl. He knew the bulge in his pants pressed to her upper leg signaled his excitement and need for her.

Hands clasped, they began their frantic flight up the stone sidewalk.

"My room," she hissed.

"Fine," he said, searching the moonlit square to be certain there was no apparent threat for them. It paid to be vigilant; especially when they both were so worked up and heady, Slocum knew he must use some caution.

"Where have you been all my life?" she asked, looking starry-eyed.

"Here and there," he said, feeling more secure and ready to make the El Grande Hotel entrance a half block away their next goal. She kissed his cheek, and they rushed forward to the open french doors, into the dimly lit lobby and up the stairs.

Halfway up the staircase, Slocum surveyed the potted palms and the sleepy-eyed desk clerk ignoring their obvious entry. Nothing looked out of place. He nodded in approval, and she held her dress up to climb to the landing. On the second floor, they hurried down the dark hall. She let go of him and fetched a key from her pocket. The lock set clicked and they were inside.

Her back to the closed door, she turned and stood on her toes to kiss him. "No lights?" she asked softly.

"No lights," he agreed and looked at the muslin curtains flowing into the room from the cooling night wind. Still on edge about their security, he kissed her again, then let go of her to check the balcony. He stepped out into the shadows and looked at the street below. Nothing appeared out of place.

"Something wrong?" she asked from inside the room.

"No, just being careful."

"Good, I had forgotten about—everything. We've had such fun tonight."

He saw that she was undoing the buttons on the front of her dress.

"It'll be all right. There's no sign of any threat to us." With the toe of his one boot he pushed off the other one and watched her undress in the shadowy light. His gunbelt hanging on a chair close by, he undid his britches, took them off and put them on the dresser. Turning back, he could make out the outline of her body as she took the camisole off over her head. The silhouette of her quaking breasts made an inviting outline.

His shirt next and he was down to his one-piece underwear. She came over and began to help him undress. They stopped to kiss and he felt her strong hands push the union suit off his shoulders. A swish of the night wind swept his bare skin, stealing some of his body heat. Her long fingers rode down his sides as if measuring him. Hands on her shoulders, he stepped out of the last layer.

They came together like starving critters, his erection against her belly. She fondled the head of it with one hand then, as if unable to wait any longer, led him to the bed. On her back, she scooted over to the center of the mattress then held out her arms for him.

Silky legs brushed against the sides of his hips, and she parted them wider and raised up for his invasion. A sharp cry of pleasure escaped her open mouth at his entry. He smiled at her wild abandonment and soft moans as they became one hard-pounding mesh. Her stomach muscles met his rip-corded ones and they sought the most of each other.

The walls of her vagina began to constrict his efforts. Her short breath roared in and out of her throat. She raised her face up so her chin was pointed at him in her effort to reach for even more pleasure. Then she clutched him like someone in deep fear of drowning and he braced himself to come.

Her cry was sharp, and he felt the blast come from deep before it flew out the end of his painfully swollen dick. The explosion pulled the plug on him and he had to brace his letdown on her, then roll aside.

"You all right?" he asked.

She rolled over to face him and mumbled, "No, I don't know where I'm at."

"Good," he said and patted her smooth, bare leg.

"It has been a long time since I felt this way," she said, getting the long hair back from her face. "I never thought I'd ever—"

"Why not? Life goes on."

"Slocum, my life has not been going on." She closed her eyes and shook her head in the room's dim light.

"Well, let's change all that." He turned over on his belly and propped himself up on his elbow.

"I'm game. When can we do this again?"

He rose up on his knees and opened her legs. Kneeling between them, he put her hand on his dick. His soldier needed no instructions, and with her subtle fingers' persuasion he soon stood at attention.

"How's that?" he asked her.

"Amazing." She snuggled downward in the bed to get him inside her nest. "Real amazing."

He smiled, lowering himself down, pushing his hard-on in her slick gates. *So are you, Amanda Debaca.*

Slocum crossed the cobblestoned way, and when he reached the doorway of the gunsmith, he turned back to look at the two familiar horses traveling down the street in his direction, their riders finding their way through the jumbled traffic of street peddlers and *carretas*. Both cowboys wore bandages over their right ears. Hats cocked to the side to accommodate the covering, they were heading north, pushing their ponies between the peddlers, goats, carts and buggies. Why, those two must be looking for some new country, Slocum decided. With a shake of his head, he entered the store that smelled of black gunpowder and oil.

"Can I help you?" a man in his forties asked, wiping down a Colt in his hand with an oily rag.

"How long will it take to put in a new trigger spring in my Colt?"

"Twenty minutes. You have the time?"

"Fine," Slocum said and drew out his Colt, unloaded the chambers and pocketed the cartridges. "I can wait."

The gunsmith checked the cylinders and examined the barrel. Then he cocked the hammer back and dry fired it. "It needs one."

"I thought so."

"Weakest link in Sam Colt's design was this spring."

Slocum nodded. Curious about the pair of departing cowboys, he wished he knew more about their experiences of the previous night. Obviously they were not headed for the hill country in the west.

"Howdy," the deputy marshal said, coming in the front door.

Slocum nodded to the man in the black suit wearing a star. The gunsmith stood up, calling the lawman by his name. "How you doing, Fred?"

"Fine. Been a helluva night. Two drifters got beat up in an alley last night and damned if whoever did it didn't cut notches in their ears."

"What for?" Slocum asked, frowning at the lawman.

"Hell, I'm not certain. The two that got notched were pretty closemouthed about their business and acted like they were in an all-fired hurry to get the hell out of San Antonio."

"Well, don't that beat all. Guess they'll wear them notches from now on," the gunsmith said, getting a handgun out of the case. "Got yours fixed. New pin was all. No charges. I don't charge the law. May need your protection."

"Well, thanks," the deputy said, holstering his piece and nodding to Slocum as he headed out the door.

"Don't that beat all?" the gunsmith asked, shaking his head over the notching incident.

Slocum agreed, busy watching the craftsman disassemble his Colt. One thing for certain, they'd damn sure be ear notched for life.

An hour later he rapped on her hotel door.

"Slocum?"

"Yes." At his reply, dressed in a bathrobe, she let him in.

"Those two rode out this morning a little worse for wear."

"They did?"

"Yes, I guess the guys who beat them up wanted to be sure they'd recognize them next time."

"How's that?"

"Marshal said that they notched their ears."

"Oh, my, you do play rough."

He shook his head, standing behind the curtain with an eye to the street below. "That wasn't my idea. But they're out of your life."

"Fine, but I must warn you, the Colonel seems to have an endless supply of their like."

"One at a time, we'll get them all notched and worked."

"Oh, no, they didn't—"

Amused, he looked at her and shook his head. "No, not this time. Who told you about me?"

"I asked some men who knew my father about you when I arrived here two days ago. They said you were the man, if I could hire you."

She was standing under him with her face thrown back. "I'm a woman without shame. I will do anything to save my ranch and those of my neighbors."

Her eyes never left his. Her fingers undid the knot in the belt on the robe. The front fell open and she put her hands on his shoulders, then she hugged him, driving her hard breasts like nails into him.

He swept her up and delivered her to the bed.

"If I can afford you—" she managed, before chuckling at his attention toward her.

Amused at her laughter, he began to take off his boots and undress, studying her well-proportioned body lying on the sheets.

"I'll never get my shopping completed—"

"My dear," he said, climbing on the bed, "that can all wait."

"I agree," she said, nesting herself on her back in the mattress.

Slocum drove the light wagon and team; his saddle horse he called Buck jogged along after tied to the tailgate. Amanda rode beside him on the spring seat, using her

parasol for shade. The drive west took the main road to
Boerne. They arrived at the village close to sundown, the
horses weary. He left her and the luggage at the one-story
hotel and drove the wagon up the street to the livery. When
he was satisfied the animals would be rubbed down,
grained and cared for, he strode up the dark street past several noisy cantinas and found her in the hotel lobby looking refreshed and smiling.

"Oh, Señora Slocum," the desk clerk said to her. "Will
you and the señor be staying longer than one night?"

"Ask my husband," she said.

He shook his head and the desk clerk nodded, satisfied.

She put on the shawl as they went out the door. "Strange
to be called Mrs. Slocum," she said, under her breath.

"Like I said earlier, it saved you the price of another
room."

She nodded with a smile. "Besides we would only use
one bed anyway." Then she hugged his arm as they crossed
the shadowy street for the restaurant.

The food was flavorful, and Slocum was eased back in
his chair when two noisy men came in the front door.
Amanda glanced over, and with a dark look on her face,
she turned back quickly to tell him, "There's two more of
them."

Slocum frowned in mild dismay. "He must have an
army."

"Hey, look what we've got us right here. If it ain't
Señora Debaca, Clyde."

The dark-haired, lanky boy of perhaps eighteen with
narrow, weak shoulders strode over to stand close to her.
He wore a six-gun with the butt pointed out on his right
hip. He was dressed in dust-floured drover's clothing, but
the expensive red rag around his neck marked him as more
than a simple cowboy. His angular face looked beardless
and his steel blue eyes held a rattlesnake's coldness that
Slocum recognized as deadly.

"Sure enough. Why, howdy, ma'am. You're sure a long ways from home, Peaches."

The second man was past thirty, with a handlebar mustache, a little thicker built than his partner. A gold watch chain swung across his gray wool vest. A thick red scar under his right eye marked his rugged pocked face, and his blue eyes carried the look of a wolf—hard and merciless.

"I'm certain you gentlemen can find places to sit," Slocum said, having already had his fill of their bald-faced openness toward her.

He saw the hint of surprise in her brown eyes at his words, like she didn't want any trouble. To calm her, he reached over and covered her hand on the table.

In a calculated move that bore his contempt, the young one thumbed his felt hat loose so it rode further back on his head. "We kinda wanted to eat with her."

She looked indignantly at Slocum, as if she would not tolerate such company.

He shook his head, first to settle her and second to answer the boy. Calm as a still glass of water, he rose and stepped close to the boy. In the flick of his wrist, he had ahold of the youth's gun hand by his forearm and his own Colt's muzzle jammed into the boy's belly.

"Did you come in here to die or what?" Slocum asked through his teeth.

"Holy Christ, who are you, mister?" Eyes big as saucers, the boy tried to look down at the gun shoved hard into his gut.

"Apologize and shake your spurs the hell out of here," Slocum ordered through his tight teeth.

"Ma'am, been a . . . a misunderstanding. Me and Clyde's leaving." Slocum released his arm and watched them, the Colt still grasped in his fist beside his right leg. Everyone in the restaurant warily watched the two as they went toward the front door.

"We was just funning," the younger one said for all to hear and then disappeared outside.

"Who was that younger one?" Slocum asked.

"Colonel Bixby's nephew, Cave." She twisted to look at the empty doorway, as if fearing their return, then turned back. "His name is Cave Bixby and the other is Clyde Wilson."

"Nice folks."

"Oh, señor, I am so sorry that those men they insulted you," the young waitress said.

"No problem." But he noted that the girl too looked frequently at the front door, as if in fear of the men's return.

"What will you have to eat?" Slocum asked Amanda.

"I'm not certain—"

"Bring us some beef and frijoles. Tortillas, too," Slocum said to get by the impasse.

"Sí," the girl said and hurried away.

"Those two will shoot you in the back," Amanda hissed, looking concerned. "They shot my husband like that."

"Maybe, maybe not."

She frowned as if deeply concerned. "Oh, I didn't ask you to defend my honor."

"Stop worrying. Their kind only understands one thing."

"What is that?"

"An iron fist." He leaned over to refill her wineglass. "Drink your wine and relax. For the moment, they're gone."

"But for how long?"

"Awhile. They aren't used to being driven off, are they?"

"No. No one is that foolish."

"Then it was time they learned better."

She shook her head, still not convinced. "If they kill you, what then?"

"Gunhands are cheap in San Antonio."

"I didn't see any when I was there."

"You didn't go in the bars where they reside. Tony could hire you a dozen like that." He snapped his fingers to make his point.

"Oh," she said and raised the glass to him. "To your health, my husband. So you live for a while."

He clinked his glass to hers. "So our life is all roses and the beds soft."

Amanda blushed and shook her head at his words.

The girl brought their food on a tray and set plates before them. "Anything else?"

"Not now," Slocum said and went to filling Amanda's dish.

"We will be at my ranch in two days. I have a room in the casa."

"I better sleep in the bunkhouse. I wouldn't want to ruin your reputation."

"Who cares?"

"You will later. We can be discreet."

"Yes," she agreed softly.

He handed her the plate of food, and she shook her head in disapproval at the size of her portions.

"Eat. We may not find such food at our next stopover."

"Aren't you thinking about those two and what they plan to do to you?" She shook her head as if amazed.

"Nothing I can do at this moment. If they're stupid, they'll try something else. Smart, they'll ride on."

"I suspect that they are out there in the street right now ready to gun you down."

"Hmm, I wonder if they have good suits with them?"

"Why?" She looked cross at him.

"Most men like to be buried in their best suits."

"Do you have one with you?"

He shook his head. "It won't be my funeral."

"I hope not," she said, and, with a look of dread, glanced at the open doorway again.

The meal complete, Slocum paid the girl, and then with his hand on Amanda's elbow he steered her swiftly through the kitchen and out the back way. "You think they're . . . ," she managed to start to ask.

His index finger silenced her. "No telling. Simply being careful."

He led the way down the alley. In the darkness, cats ran for cover and the smell of refuse was strong. The alley opened to a street and he forced her to stand in the shadows close to the wall.

"I'll be right back."

He eased himself up on the stone sidewalk and under a canopy. Step by step, he slipped along the darkened front of a store. He could make out the familiar hat on the individual leaning with his shoulder to the next building. All of the man's attention was centered on the lighted doorway of the cafe.

Slocum drew his Colt, stepped behind the unsuspecting man and slashed him on the back of the head. He went down with barely an audible grunt. Where was Wilson? Careful to watch for any movement or threat, Slocum knelt down, swept up Bixby's sidearm and jammed it in his waistband. He felt certain Bixby would have a severe headache in the morning.

Not seeing Wilson, he backtracked, took Amanda by the arm and then went the opposite direction. Soon they were inside the hotel.

"What happened back there?" she asked, looking relieved when they were in the lobby.

"That Bixby boy is sleeping in the alley."

She put her hand to her mouth to control her chuckles. "Oh, did he surrender his pistol, too?" She indicated the butt sticking out from behind his waistband.

"Not voluntarily, but he did. And I could have notched his ears, too, but I didn't."

"Ow." She made a shudder of disgust and drew out the room key.

"Hey, you'd recognize him that way." He glanced around to be certain they were alone. Nothing.

"Where was his partner?"

"I never saw him."

She swung the door open. The night wind fluttered the muslin curtains. Swiftly, he went to check and see if there was anyone out there. In a minute, after his eyes adjusted to the night and he could make out the scene, he felt satisfied there was no threat.

"I'll fix the bed," she offered.

"No, we'll make a pallet on the floor," he said. "Sorry, but I won't like being shot to death in a bed."

"Oh—" She clapped a hand to her mouth.

"Just to be on the safe side."

"Oh, yes."

He put her close to the wall on the blanket they would share, his Colt beside him on the floor. They kissed, and she turned to lie on her side, facing the wall.

"I have gotten you in a mess," she said, sounding concerned.

"No, you're in one and we're going to extract you from it."

"Oh, I hope so."

Slocum awoke and listened. Something had jarred him from his slumber. He had been sleeping light anyway. His fingers closed on the redwood grips of the six-gun. He turned an ear to hear better. If they were out there—they better have their funeral bills paid.

Then he heard the ring of a spur not far from the window and he sat up. Whoever was out there was stupid enough to wear them to his own funeral. The outline of a pistol soon came past the curtains and the Colt in Slocum's hand came alive. A red muzzle blast and a scream in the night—Slocum charged to his feet and was to the window in a flash. He could see someone was on the ground, moaning. Slocum could make out another's outline on horseback, twenty steps away, holding the second horse.

His Colt drawn up and sighted, it barked a red flash in the night. But the clatter of hooves told him enough—the rider was getting away in the darkness. Slocum stepped out the window for a better look and to be certain the downed one was unarmed.

"I'm hit bad," Bixby cried when Slocum kicked his pistol away.

"You're lucky," he said, seeing someone with a lamp coming out the rear door of the hotel.

"What happened out here?"

"Get the law. A man tried to kill us in our bed."

"Oh—" The person with the lamp ran back inside.

"You all right?" Amanda asked in a sleep-filled voice from inside the window.

"Yes—fine. Go back to sleep. They've gone for the law."

"How?" She climbed over the low windowsill and wrapped the robe tighter around her. "Who is it?"

"Bixby."

"I'm dying, ma'am."

"Oh."

"Shut up," Slocum said. "Where did your pal go?"

"How am I . . . to know that?"

"What's going on back here?" someone of authority demanded.

"You the law?"

"Yes, I'm the marshal."

"This guy's hit. He tried to kill me and her while we slept."

"I'm dying," Bixby moaned.

"Hmm, what did he try that for?"

"Better ask him."

"You'll have plenty of time to die," the marshal said, looking over the dark faces cautiously gathering in the alley. "Couple of you grab him and take him to the jail. Monroe?"

"Yeah, Sam?"

"Go get the doc. Have him meet us at the jail." The lawman turned and faced them. "Sorry, was there more than him?"

"Yes, the other one rode off when the shooting broke loose."

"Come by the office before you leave town, sir. I didn't catch your name?"

"Slocum's my name."

"Sam Haze's mine."

They shook hands and Slocum led Amanda back to the window.

"All right, clear out," the marshal said to the onlookers as three men carted off the wounded Bixby.

"Oh, I was so afraid," Amanda said, burying her face on Slocum's chest when they were alone again in the room.

"We're fine. We can even sleep on the bed this time," he said to soothe her.

"What about—"

"Wilson won't dare come back. Let's get some sleep." They'd need their rest. There would be two more days on the road to reach her ranch.

4

"Señor! Señor!"

Bixby tried to clear his head. What loco jackass was pounding on his bedroom door? He looked over at the frightened brown eyes of the girl Edora hugging the sheet to hide her nakedness.

"Stay there," he said to her in disgust.

He waded across the room to the door with a blanket wrapped around his flank. "What is it?"

"Your nephew, he is shot."

"Huh?" He jerked open the door and glared at the older woman standing there. "Where is he?"

"In jail in Boerne. Wilson send word that Señor Cave was badly shot, señor."

"Where's Wilson at?" he roared at her.

"Gone." She held up her palms. "I know nothing more. They say Wilson, he ran for the border."

"What the hell did they do, for Christ's sake?"

"I don't know."

"Fix my breakfast and send word to the bunkhouse I want two men to ride with me in thirty minutes."

"Sí, señor." The old woman hurried off down the hall, as if glad to be sent away.

Bixby blundered back into the room. He looked at the cowering girl holding the sheet and then dismissed her. Instead of messing with her tight pussy, he better get dressed and learn about his nephew's welfare. Who in the hell shot him? Whoever did it would damn sure pay.

He pulled on his pants and roared like a lion at her. "Get me some clean socks!"

She hurried to obey as he put on his shirt. What in the hell had that stupid horny boy gotten himself into? The dumb ass, anyway.

5

The live-oak- and cedar-clad rolling hill country spread out
before them. Slocum drove the matched team at a hard jog
and his bay saddle pony came along behind the spring
wagon. Amanda under her parasol sat to his left, so the six-
gun riding on his right hip was less encumbered. Before
him in the scabbard on the dashboard was the loaded .44-
40 Winchester he'd traded for before leaving Boerne, to be
jerked up in case of an attack.

They splashed through the small spring-fed creeks and
drove up the other side. Pretty time of year, he decided.
There would be a light frost in the next thirty days, but
winters were always mild in the hill country. Compared to
Montana or Oregon, this was banana land.

"Tell me about Slocum," she said.

"Not much to tell. I came from Alabama, fought in a
gray uniform, and after the war I drifted west."

"Never married? Never engaged?"

"Age when mostly folks were doing that, I was off fighting the war."

"Never even were engaged?"

He shook his head. He explained how at sixteen, his life
on the family plantation was as close to heaven as anyone

could get. Good horses, real treeing hounds, dancing with pretty girls at house parties and learning about the mysteries of womanhood from the black house help. My, my, a boy could get lots of lessons from some hatch-assed wench. At age seventeen, he was wearing a uniform. Before his eighteenth birthday, he watched his best buddy's head explode when he was hit by some grenade shrapnel.

Four years of war left him spent, without purpose, and he returned to the ravaged ruins of the home place. Sherman had burned her to the ground. His mother dead. His father, only a shell of the man he'd left. It was over the land taxes the carpetbaggers slapped on the place. He killed one of them when he came to foreclose. That forced Slocum to ride away. But he was no stranger to avoiding those after him—he'd done that for years.

He was holed up on the Cherokee Reservation in the Nation. Lots of Southern sympathy in those people. General Stande Waitie and others had fought for the South. Slocum soon found the trustworthy ones and how to tell who were the Pins, who worked for the Union Army.

It was near the Grand River. A Cherokee woman, Rose Many Tree, owned a small ranch, and they went there to help her gather some hogs. Late in the fall, the colorful hardwoods were fast shedding their coat of brown, red and gold.

The name of the other white boy who rode up there with him was Ivan Groom. Dark brown headed, they were both wiry and lanky. In fact, Rose asked them when they rode up if they were brothers. Just there by happenstance—they'd heard she needed some help.

A woman in her mid-thirties, her skin was darker than a copper penny. Facial features too sharp to be handsome, but her coal black eyes and the smiles she gave them while they talked to her made her a pleasing-looking person. Willowy figure in the wash-worn dress, she went and found some whiskey after she told them how she wanted them to do this hog catching on the shares and they agreed.

Rose never mentioned a man, or if she'd ever had one. Slocum didn't bother to mention this part of the story to Amanda, but if the chance came along either him or Ivan would have plied on top of Rose and screwed her till she was too sore to walk.

They had some luck early on in the hog hunting—they caught ten head in a log trap. Five of the pigs bore her ear mark, and three others, the owner Pete Dead Horse came by when she summoned him and gave them three dollars apiece for them. They turned the last two out. Pete didn't know the mark, so they released them.

They invested ten dollars in a catch dog, and he put them in the hog-getting business. A half bulldog, he could grab an ear and hang on to the squealing pig till they could scramble through the winter-bare hardwoods, vines and saw briars and tie their catch up.

Merve Thunder came by Rose's place one night asking if they'd seen his big boar. They were sitting up late playing cards with her. While he didn't divulge this information to Amanda either, Slocum always considered him and Ivan real lucky to have found this job, because by dark most nights, one or two of the boys had Rose up in the four-poster bed, banging hard on her ass.

"He's mostly red and weighs over three hundred pounds," Thunder said. "Got a fork in his right ear and three slashes in his left. I get him up, I'll cut his balls out and feed him corn for two moons, make a lot of damn good pork for my family."

Rose laughed. "Them Merry boys got a leg broke cutting a boar that big last year."

"Shit fire, Rose, them dumb boys could screw up a good thing."

"They ain't too smart, are they?" She smiled, amused about those Merry boys' intelligence.

The next day, a northern blew in and they stomped around Rose's stove till mid-morning before going pig hunting. An hour out, they spotted a big red hog cutting down off a mountainside and set their dog and horses in after it.

"Woo dog! Woo dog!" Ivan shouted as they rode over persimmon and hickory saplings, bearing down on the big critter.

The dog, Bull, got the idea and he tore like a shot off through the post oaks on the hillside after the runaway. They had to whip their ponies to keep up. Twice they caught sight of the king pig, but he was a cagey one.

Then Bull went to baying, and soon the damndest screams came from ahead.

"Bull's got him eared," Ivan shouted and Slocum agreed. They whipped and rode hard until they found the dog and hog in the Grand River. Trouble was the large boar had the best of the ear-gripping dog and he was under the surface. Ivan never slowed down; he drove his horse off in the thick, ice-edged water and dove in to save old Bull's life.

Slocum got out his lariat and pushed his horse into the river after the hog. He made a good loop and caught the front quarters and one front leg of the surging boar. Slocum dallied his rope on the horn and sent his pony for the bank. On the land, the angry, wild boar charged Slocum and his boogered horse until at last Slocum got him tied to a thorny tree and rode over to see how Ivan was doing.

Soaked to the skin, Ivan was shaking so hard his teeth were rattling, but he was trying to build a fire. Slocum took over the job and had things going in a few minutes. They were over an hour's hard ride from the cabin and Slocum worried he might die of exposure in that long of a ride. But the sharp wind and low temperatures never let him warm up. His wet clothes froze. He finally decided it would be best for them to ride for Rose's.

He raced the horses home and delivered the shivering

Ivan to her. She stripped off his ice-stiff clothing and forced him on the bed, then she stripped and told Slocum to cover them up with all the blankets in the cabin as she huddled her naked body against his chilled-to-the-bone form.

Ivan never warmed, until he took pneumonia two days later. He shivered under all the quilts they could pile on him, plus Rose's fierce body heat. Then the fever came and replaced the chills. Six days after he dove in the Grand River to save Bull, Ivan went to his reward, delirious and congested to death.

"I'll make him a grave," Slocum said.

Rose held her hand out to stop him. "Ain't you wanted by them federal marshals in Van Buren?" she asked. "Now poor Ivan, he's dead. But he looks enough like you I say take him down there and get the reward on Slocum. They's ain't got no pitchers of you, have they?"

"No, but it sounds awful mean, and cruel."

"That boy woulda give his life for you like he did that dog. He won't've cared no way where they buried him."

So Slocum rode the hard, frozen military road to Van Buren, Arkansas, and told the desk man in Judge Story's courthouse that he had a wanted man's body outside belly-down over a horse.

"Who is it?" the fat-faced man asked, not looking up from the papers he was stamping.

"John Slocum."

"What's he wanted for?"

"Killing some federal man in Alabama."

"How you know you got him?"

Slocum pulled off his mittens and dug out a wanted poster. It was worn on the creases, but he unfolded and smoothed it before him. The man raised his eyes up to look at it. "John . . . Slo-cum all right. How you know you got him?"

"He told me his name 'fore he died."

"You shoot him?" the man asked, back at his stamping again and not looking up.

"No, he died of pneumonia."

"I've got to be damn sure before I pay any federal reward."

"Here." Slocum handed over the last two letters his mother had wrote him, before she died. "These was on him."

The man looked them over and then returned his gaze to Slocum. "Guess he was John Slocum, all right. What's your name?"

"Ivan Broom."

"Well, Mr. Broom, you're forty dollars richer if that guy out there is John Slocum."

"It's him all right."

"Take him to the undertaker down the street, get a receipt for John Slocum and come right back up here."

Slocum put his gloves back on. Damn cold had locked up the whole country. The Arkansas River was frozen thick enough they told him he could ride his horse across it and never fall through the ice.

Slocum delivered the body to Weir, Weir and Naylor's funeral home. The big man who worked there went out and shouldered Ivan's body off the horse and carried it into the parlor by himself, with Slocum opening and closing doors for him. The blue-faced body was laid out on a marble slab in the back room. Slocum waited for the man to go back into the heated portion of the building. Their breath was making clouds of fog in the morgue.

"Bet that outlaw will be glad to go to hell, cold as it is here," the big man said, filling out the receipt at his desk.

Slocum nodded in agreement.

"John Slocum, huh? He was a killer?"

"I guess. He said he shot a federal tax man in Alabama."

"Hmm," Weir said. "Ought to give him a marble monument for doing that, huh?"

"I don't know, sir."

"I do." He signed off on the receipt and handed it to Slocum.

The paper in his coat pocket, Slocum put on his gloves. "You know anyone needs a good horse?"

Weir shook his head. "I don't. Have to feed him till spring."

That might be a long ways off, too. Slocum left. The secretary at the court told him he could give him a warrant for the forty dollars, but it wouldn't be paid until Congress made the next appropriation of money for the court.

"What do I do?" Slocum asked, confused why the richer-than-hell U.S. government didn't have the money to pay him.

"There's folks will discount it around town. Oh, you should get twenty-five for it."

"Twenty-five dollars? But the reward said forty."

"I told you, you'll have to wait until Congress . . . Do I look like I run Congress? No. When they allocate the money, then your warrant will be worth forty dollars."

"When're they going to advocate that money?" Besides anger over the possible wait, Slocum felt confused about why he wasn't getting the total amount promised.

"November—oh, probably March, or it may be before they recess in July, this ain't no election year."

"All right." Slocum surrendered. "Who discounts them?"

"Mr. Dover at the First National Bank. Mark Dannier at the Van Buren Mercantile."

"Yes," Slocum said and wanted to know what this clerk got out of the deal. The whole thing about not paying him the full cash amount looked fixed to him.

"Find some more outlaws, dead or alive, bring them in, boy."

Slocum nodded that he'd heard him and went back out in the cold. The howling wind swept ice particles off the porch into his face. He left the hipshot horses at the rack and walked the half block to the bank. Inside the bank, Slocum waited his turn, seated on a wood bench, and when at last he was ushered into the banker's office, he found a red-nosed man with gold wire frames who was willing to pay him $27.50 for his warrant.

"Congress may not pay this till next summer. You understand I must be careful. You drive a hard bargain for a man so young." He was overseeing Slocum writing his name on the back: Ivan Broom.

"Would you like to deposit this money in my bank, Mr. Broom?" Red Nose asked.

"No, sir, I've got bills to pay."

"I see. Here's your money, sir." He counted it out on the polished desktop and Slocum shoved it deep in his pockets.

"Who buys horses?" he asked the man.

He shook his head. "They're hard to sell this time of year."

"Everything's hard to sell around here," Slocum said in disgust and left Van Buren.

When Slocum finished his story, Amanda nodded and smiled at him. "Some story." He drew up the team in the bright midday sun to let them drink from the stream. Brake set, he tied off the reins.

"So you aren't wanted any longer?" she asked.

He paused, ready to get down. "Not by the federal marshals."

"Oh."

"There's another story I'll tell you later."

A shot rang out, and in an instant he reached for her, catching her by the waist, and swept her off the seat to put her down on the gravel. The far horse in her team reared when a second bullet thumped hard into him. The animal screamed and fell over in the harness as Slocum jerked the Winchester out and levered in a shell, trying to tell from what direction the shots were coming.

"Stay down," he warned her, desperately searching the thick cedars for a sight of the shooter.

"Oh, god, they've shot Big Man."

"Stay down. He's still out there."

Then the sound of hoofbeats racing away were all he could hear besides the wind rustling the live oak and swishing through the cedar boughs. It was a lonely place to ambush anyone on purpose. Couldn't get a clear shot at them either for all the brush, so instead he shot one of their horses. *Wilson, you bastard.*

"He ride off?"

"I'm not sure. Stay on the ground."

"What will we do now?" she asked.

"Hook Buck up," he said.

"He broke to harness?"

"He will be by the time we get to your place." He laid the rifle on the wagon floor.

"Perhaps you'll wish you'd never seen me," she said in a small girl's voice.

"No, my dear. You've been the bright star in this matter since I met you." He helped her up, still wary, but convinced that the shooter had run away.

"I can't see how," she said and brushed the dirt from her dress tail.

"You are," he repeated. How was Buck going to take to harness? They'd know in a few minutes. He would need to get the bloody horse out of the harness and try it on Buck. That might be a real new deal.

Bent over, he began to unbuckle and unharness the dead horse. Then he took the live one off the tongue and led him over to the shade to rest. She brought Buck over there for him. In places, Slocum strained to pull the rigging out from under the dead horse. Old Buck better like this new job. They were still a day and a half away from her ranch.

At last the saddle horse was harnessed and both horses

hooked to the wagon. Slocum clucked to the new team. Buck reared and then plunged forward. The steady horse on the inside didn't let Buck's foolishness spook him, and they rode off with Buck pulling the entire wagon load and the inside horse holding back enough to let him do all the work.

Rafterville was a sleepy place, with a few stores and three cantinas. The storekeeper who came out the front door, scratching his belly through his soiled white apron, leaned on the porch post and told them, "Howdy."

"Anyone been through here in the last hour?" Slocum asked.

"A rider going west."

"Know him?"

The man shook his head. "Never seen him before in my life. Drifter, he looked like most of them."

"Someone shot one of the lady's horses." Slocum jumped down, then helped Amanda off the spring seat. "You got a livery here?"

"Down there." The man indicated with his thumb, then made a half bow for Amanda. "Ma'am, anything you need in my humble establishment, I'd be more than glad to find it for you. That is if I've got it in stock."

"While you're doing that, I'll go see about another horse," Slocum said to her and clucked to the team.

She nodded that she had heard him, then put on her best face for the merchant. "I do need a few things."

Slocum traded for a black horse that about matched Amanda's other one. The livery man hadn't seen anyone pass through. So with the new team in place, Slocum hitched Buck to the tailgate and drove back to the store.

"Thank you, Mr. Canton," she said and handed Slocum the poke of food and items she'd purchased to put in back. Slocum gave her a hand up.

"Ma'am, I'm right put out that sorry outfit shot your good hoss." Canton scratched his belly through his shirt. "In a case like that he needs to be strung up."

"He needs a lesson," she agreed. "Good day, sir."

"Thanks again, ma'am." He waved and Slocum drove off.

"Well, I have coffee, some beans to boil, bacon, some flour, baking soda and lard, and can make some bread. His meat looked a little aged."

"Well, ma'am . . . ," Slocum said in imitation of Canton's bass voice, and they both laughed.

She glanced back, then turned forward. "He was a character. We should be at Corral Springs by tomorrow."

"Can we make your place from there in a day?"

"Oh, yes."

"So we have one more night under the stars?"

She hugged his arm. "I usually look forward to arriving home. This time I may not be so sure."

"Are there children?"

"No, we never could have any of our own. But I'll have to again think about the ranch and the people who work for me and the problems. I have been on a big absence from my business, and the things that usually worry me all the time have vaporized since I've been with you." She put her forehead against him. "It has been a nice few days save for all the shooting."

He looked off at the hills ahead. "I can't stay forever. Someday I'll have to leave you—without warning."

"But I thought that you had all the wanted poster problems solved?"

He clucked to the horses to keep them moving. "A few years after that, in Fort Scott, Kansas, a boy of eighteen tried to egg me into a gunfight over his losses at cards. I threw him out the door, and he came back armed and shot at me. To make a long story short, his father was a wealthy man; he owned the sheriff, judge and jury. There's a murder warrant up there for my arrest and he keeps two Kansas deputies on my backtrail."

"But it was in self-defense—"

"Too much water's gone under the bridge. I just keep moving. They aren't particularly smart, but they hound me."

"What if something happened to them?"

He shook his head and slapped the lazy black horse on the butt with the lines. "Then he might hire real dogs that bite."

"I see what you mean." She smiled. "I'm ready to camp for the night. There's a good place about two miles ahead."

"Guess you like sleeping out under the stars as well as you do sleeping in a bed."

"I do, Slocum, with you." She nodded smugly and squeezed his arm. "You have spoiled me. I never thought I'd ever meet a man who would turn me into such an uninhibited flossy as you have."

They both laughed. He was thinking about this Colonel Bixby and his bunch and her troubles with them. He still owed Wilson for killing her horse.

6

Rainbows shone in the droplets of water she threw by the handful at him. As she stood knee deep in the flowing stream, the late-afternoon sun glistened on her olive skin. The dark rings of her pointed nipples were puckered by the water's cold temperature. Her face showed every intention of her dampening him with efforts at splashing water. Then in a final charge, he rushed inside her defenses and took her in his arms.

Lips clung to lips. The overpowering need for each other smothered out all the excitement of seconds before and swept over both of them as their water-slick bodies meshed in each other's arms and they sought to become one.

He swept her off her feet in his arms and headed for the shore.

"Put me down . . ." Her mouth smothered his and her tongue tasted his.

"Not until—" He turned an ear to listen to something he'd heard. The distant drum of horse hooves caused him to set her down.

They were far enough off the road—still, he motioned for her to head for their clothing, and followed close behind on her heels. He swept up the Winchester. By the time they reached the cedars, she was struggling into her dress.

"Who—"

"I'm not certain. But our wagon tracks going up here are obvious enough to see from the road." He noticed that their grazing horses were looking north at the unseen intruders.

Out of breath, and working her dress down, she joined him. He handed her the rifle and quickly pulled on his britches.

"They're still coming?" she asked, with her head turned, trying to hear.

His arms in his shirt, he listened keenly. Men were talking in the direction of the road. No doubt they'd discovered the wagon tracks that turned downstream. Then he heard someone shout, "This way."

He took the repeater back from her and checked the chamber, then drew the butt to his shoulder. In a few seconds, they burst into camp.

"It's him—Bixby," she hissed.

Slocum nodded.

"Whoa! Look about for them," the tall figure on a dun horse shouted.

"Drop those guns!" Slocum ordered. His first round took the hat off the big man's head and he levered in a new round.

The three wide-eyed men dropped their six-shooters and threw up their hands. The one she called Bixby had turned beet red with anger.

"Who in the hell're you?" Bixby demanded.

"The man who's going to send you to hell. Where do you get off riding into a man's camp, guns drawn and looking for trouble?"

"You killed my nephew?"

"Mister, that boy came looking to die." Slocum by this time could see that Wilson wasn't with them. "And that other ranny of yours named Wilson shot one of her horses. Guess you'll pay for that."

"What the hell you talking about?"

"Act dumb, but dig out her forty dollars. Wilson's on your payroll." By this time, he had figured that the two with Bixby weren't much of a threat. One wore a mustache, the other needed a shave; he considered neither of them tough as the Colonel. In fact, he figured he could tie a tin can to their tails and send them packing quicker than a cat could switch its tail.

"I ain't paying for no damn horse."

"Wilson works for you. He's the back-shooter that couldn't hit a bull in the ass, and shot her horse. I expect you to pay for it."

"I don't know your name."

"Keep your damn hands in the sky," Slocum said as Amanda picked up the last handgun and came back with her collection to the wagon. "You don't need my name, mister, you just need to know there's other folks in this country that got a right to be here besides yourself."

"I'll get you." Bixby narrowed his eyes in anger.

"Don't be making threats. You ain't in any position to do that."

"I'll—"

"You'll be filling a buzzard's guts if'n you don't keep them hands up."

"You've made a big mistake coming here, boy. I don't know what that Messikan bitch told you—"

"Get off that horse!" Bixby's words had sent hot jolts of rage up Slocum's jaw.

"Huh—"

"Get off that horse." Slocum reinforced his threat by jabbing him in the ribs with his rifle muzzle.

"Here," he said to Amanda, handing over the rifle. "Shoot them if they decide to run away."

"He'll kill you," she whispered, realizing Slocum's intentions, her deep concern mirrored in her brown eyes.

"I don't think so." When Slocum stepped toward the big man, he wished he'd had time to put on his boots. The sticks were jabbing his bare soles as he moved about.

A broad smile spread over Bixby's full face. He rubbed a big fist in the palm of his left hand. Satisfaction danced in his blue eyes. A look of smugness swept his full mouth.

Slocum drove in hard. His first three blows to the man's cheekbones sent him reeling backward, though he threw some wild swings. Bixby managed to land a glancing blow to Slocum's shoulder, but took two hard hits under his eyes that staggered him.

"You're going to learn some manners this evening," Slocum said, dodging a wild haymaker and nailing in two more quick fists to Bixby's head.

"About what?"

"About who you call a bitch."

"Ha, her—"

Slocum's fist pounded his nose, and Bixby ducked back, slinging blood. "I'll call that bitch a bitch—"

"Not while I'm around." Filled with a newfound fury, Slocum moved in and in five punches had the big man sprawled on his back. He stood over him, ready for any attempt by him to get up.

Bixby shook his head, stunned, and then tried to rise, but never made it. Blood ran in streams from both his nostrils, over his mouth, and he spit some of it.

"I ever hear you call her bitch again, I'll whip you with my pistol."

"You ain't heard the last of this."

"You want more?"

"No."

"Then shut up. Bixby, you aren't driving any more folks out of this country."

The big man never answered. Slocum stepped over and jerked him up by the collar until it threatened to choke him. "Dig out that forty dollars for the horse Wilson shot."

"The hell—" His words cut off when Slocum's boot toe caught him in the gut and threw him down on his back.

"All right—" Bixby managed, as he drew out a wallet and put the money on the ground.

"You two," Slocum shouted at the riders when he'd swept up the cash. "Get off your horses and help him on his. Next time, you two bring shovels."

"What for?" the mustached one asked.

"So you can bury the son of a bitch."

The two struggled to put their boss on his horse. They kept glancing back, giving Amanda and Slocum the shifty-eyed look. When at last they had the groaning Bixby in the saddle, Slocum laughed out loud.

"If you two boys don't want your ears notched like Taker and Nichols got theirs done for them in San Antonio, you better take a big powder out of this country after today."

They never answered, but plenty of white showed around their eyes before they hit their own saddles and, leading the bent-over, groaning Bixby, headed for the road.

"You've hurt your hand?" Amanda asked with the rifle in the crook of her arm.

Slocum shook his head, watching the threesome disappear around some cedars. His fists did hurt, but aside from some skinned knuckles, they'd be all right.

"You know you have really provoked him."

Slocum nodded, the anger still draining from him.

"My husband did that, too."

He nodded that he'd heard her. Her husband was dead, too.

7

"What the hell happened to you?" McKlein asked. "Damn, you get kicked by a mule?" The lawman walked around Bixby's desk, looking hard at the man, then poured himself some whiskey.

"You know this sumbitch she hired named Slocum?"

"No, but he beat up and ear-notched two of your men in San Antonio."

"Nichols and Taker?"

"Yeah, them two. I got word late yesterday he fixed them, or someone that works for him did it."

"How many men has he got?" Bixby shook his head. The sumbitch was alone when he jumped him.

"No telling." McKlein took a seat and studied the liquor in his glass.

"What the hell we going to do about him?"

"Why don't I arrest him for murder?"

"Fine with me, but how—"

"He won't ever make it to jail." McKlein gave a smug look at the whiskey then took a big drink of the contents.

"That's the best plan yet. My men ran off all her stock up on that creek. Said that they ran them to kingdom come."

47

"Good, she'll have to give up before long. Did she try to see the Rangers while she was there?"

"My contact said no. Since they never answered her telegrams, she probably gave up, huh? Shame they never got them messages, huh?"

Bixby's face hurt like a festered boil when he agreed with a nod. He'd get that damn Slocum. The vision in his right eye was still blurry, and the lids barely parted enough to see light. Damn him.

"I've got to hire some more deputies," McKlein said.

"What for?"

"So she don't send any word out. Need more guards on all the main roads."

"Hire them."

"Cost thirty a month per man."

"How many men?"

"Six, two on each road."

"Here's two hundred a month." Bixby took the gold coins from the center drawer in his desk and piled them up. "Be damn sure they don't let anyone out that could get word to the Rangers."

McKlein picked up the coins. "I been doing the job, ain't I?"

"Yeah. Now arrest that sumbitch."

"I'll handle Slocum."

Bixby stood by the window and watched McKlein ride out. One more matter handled.

8

Slocum reined up the team and from the distance studied Amanda's ranch headquarters before they began their descent to the valley floor. The two-story house that rose over the smattering of adobe structures and corrals reminded him of the haciendas of Mexico. Hemmed in by the limestone bluffs, the creek bottomland shone golden brown, with rolling acres of a good corn crop on the stalks.

"*Mi casa*," she said with a smile.

"Pretty place," he said and clucked to the team.

Dogs began to bark as they came up the lane between the cornfields. Rail-and-post fences lined their way.

"You'll have a wonderful corn crop," he said to her.

"Yes, but I have many to feed."

Several women came running, and bashful, dark-eyed children were holding back, but they spied on the two of them. In colorful dresses, from the attractive to grandmotherly, the women of the ranch all looked excited at the return of their patron.

"Señora, Señora," they cried, acting pleased to see her.

"This is Señor Slocum," she announced. They bowed their heads then smiled at him. "He has come to help us."

"What happened to your other horse?" one of the older women asked, looking at the black one.

"Someone shot him."

"Do you know who?"

She turned to Slocum. "A man called Wilson."

"Ah, he works for the Colonel," the woman said. Others with hatred in their eyes nodded that they, too, knew the man.

"But Señor Slocum made the Colonel pay for the horse," she said to them.

An "oh" came in approval from the women.

"What has happened while I have been gone, Margarita?" she asked one of the older women.

"They ran your cattle out of the Rio Bianco land."

"Where are the men?" Amanda frowned at her, searching around for sight of them.

The woman folded her arms and drew her head erect. "Trying to gather all those cattle they chased away."

"I have a deed to that place," Amanda said to Slocum.

"Who ran them out?" He looked over the women for an answer.

"Who does everything bad around here?" Margarita said.

Slocum nodded. He needed to learn more about Bixby and his total operation. "Do you have a map?"

"Yes, in the house." Amanda turned back. "How's Mena's baby?"

"Doing better," Margarita said.

"Good. I want the men to meet Slocum when they return."

"*Sí, señora.* I will send them to the house."

"Good. Let's go inside and find some lunch," she said to Slocum.

"Fine," he said and followed her over the limestone walk to the front door.

"Pepe, take care of the señor's horse, too," she shouted to the youth ready to drive off the team.

"Ah, *sí.*"

Slocum smiled at her. "These people have been here on this place a long time."

"Yes, my grandfather was here when the first Americanos came to San Antonio. He knew them well, Travis and Sam Houston, and fought against Santa Anna's forces for Texas as I told you."

"And you are the last of the line?"

She nodded slightly. "My husband and I prayed for children. You would have liked him. He was a good man—half and half. His mother was from Tennessee and his father was Mexican."

"Tell me again how he was killed."

"Shot in the back. No one we know saw it—perhaps only the killer was there—"

"No, these buzzards travel in pairs or more. Two in San Antonio, and Bixby came with two more. If someone shot your husband, then I'd bet good money that someone saw it happen."

"But how will we get them to talk? The sheriff is no help."

They stopped to wash their hands at the pitcher and bowl in the hallway. She motioned for him to go ahead. She used her teeth to remove her goatskin gloves. His hands washed and his sun-heated face rinsed down, he dried himself on the towel and watched her. The woman was pleasant to look at despite the road dust and travel wear; she still maintained a certain aura about her that he liked.

She finished and motioned for him to follow her.

The long dining table was as he'd expected. Two women were standing at ready beside the door he decided led to the kitchen.

"Bring some wine and food," Amanda said to them.

"*Sí, señora*. Good to have you home. You too, señor." They both hurried out of the room.

"These people speak lots of English," he said, showing her to her chair.

"We are Texans. We are Americans. Our children here go to school."

"I understand that. Your enemy ran off your cattle. Well, someone did. That's strange that no one has made them stop. The law, the Rangers?" He took a seat. Corrupt local officials were one thing, but the Rangers had always been the force that ran off the Indians and shut down the corrupt politicians.

He took his seat and the younger girl filled his glass with a red wine. *"Gracias, señorita,"* he said, putting his cloth napkin in his lap.

"You are welcome, señor."

He nodded and shared a private look with Amanda. They were Americans. "When did you last try to contact the Rangers?"

She shook her head. "I have telegraphed for the Rangers three times and they did not come."

"I know some Rangers. I'll wire one first time I get to town."

"You must be careful. Take some men with you where you go. After the way you beat him up, he will for sure try to kill you." She snapped her fingers to show him how quick Bixby would respond. The anger in her eyes flared like a fire doused with coal oil.

Slocum agreed and they ate their lunch of tasty strips of marinated beef, frijoles and fresh tortillas. When they'd finished, he smiled at her. "Let's look over your maps."

She nodded and rose, then led him into a side room and pointed to the map on the wall. "These are my holdings. That is where the men are at, trying to gather back the cattle." Her finger for a pointer, she showed him the boundaries and the water course. "Bonito Creek is a very strong one. Even in a dry year, the springs flow."

"And this is Bixby's land?" he asked, looking at the bordering portion.

"Yes."

"I see his problem. You have the water and he doesn't."

"He could develop water. Since my grandfather's time we have opened springs on our other places, and we have dependable water there, too."

"Ah, once again you control the water."

She frowned in disapproval at him. "My father could have owned that land, but he considered it too rough to utilize for grazing."

"Amanda, you don't understand. All that Bixby wants is your water."

"But—"

He hugged her shoulder and laughed. "Greed, my dear, can be a deep thing for men like him."

"What can I do?"

"Kill him in the end."

"Kill him?" Her thick, dark lashes fluttered at his words.

"Either that or destroy him. He won't quit short of his goal to force you out of here."

"Then let's kill him. An eye for an eye, no?"

"Let me try to discourage him first."

"What will you do?"

"I'm not sure yet. Is there a boy here on the ranch that could guide me?"

"I am sure that Montez can get you the best one. He should be here by evening."

"Wonderful. Now you can show me the layout of this place."

"The house?"

"Later." He smiled at her. "I mean the corrals and buildings."

"Surely."

She took him around to the various quarters for the families, the pens and the blacksmith shop. He met the ranch's resident smithy, a well-muscled man called Cortez who was busy making horseshoes in his forge. He gave a few pumps on his large bellows that sent the sharp aroma of burning coal in the air, then stripped off his glove to shake Slocum's hand.

"Señor Slocum, this is Cortez."

A few words were exchanged and they went by the saddlery, where an ancient man with gnarled fingers wove a riata from strands of rawhide. The sharply defined smell of lanoline hung in the air as he dappled his fingers in a dish of it to soften the stiff rawhide and make the finished lariat pliable. He gave them a toothless grin and a nod.

"Carlos is the best braider in the West," Amanda bragged. "Next year he will be ninety-two. Still a young man, no?" she said to Slocum. The old man grinned, pleased at her words.

"Good to meet you," Slocum said to him in Spanish.

The old man said in return, "Gracias," busy crossing and working tight his efforts.

Extra saddles were on the wall racks. Bridles and sets of harness were all oiled and well cared for. The ranch was a tight operation; he noted the fine horses in the corrals. They were sleek and well bred, not ordinary mustangs, but the product of selection and a breeding program.

The place had an outer perimeter of rock walls from the days of the Comanche raids. But the gates were gone after many years without usage.

"We need to post guards on the gates," he said.

"You don't think—"

"I think so far they've failed in their attempts to run you off. They killed your husband, they've run your stock off, and you have not left or offered to sell them your ranch."

"Of course not."

"Then we must defend the place from attack."

"How?" she asked as they headed for the house with her nodding and speaking to various women on their way. Children ran about playing, and their laughter rang in the air.

"We need the gates blocked with wagons or *carretas* at night, so they can't charge in here like they own the place. Second, an armed man at each gate. High up, so he can duck behind the wall but see for a long ways anyone approaching. We may want to cut and burn some trees out there that would afford them close-by cover."

"You really expect a raid here, don't you?"

"I would rather be ready than sorry later."

"That is why I hired you." She shook her head. "But raid my ranch—I can't believe it."

"A raid wouldn't bother him one bit."

She clasped his arm. "Slocum, I can't thank you enough."

"Oh, you might."

"Oh." She checked the sun time, then lowered her voice. "We have time before the men return for us to work on it."

"And spoil my siesta?"

She poked him hard in the ribs. "I'll spoil it all right."

He studied some gathering clouds. He needed next to see Bixby's operation, then plan his own trickery—there would be a way to make the Colonel's days unpleasant in return. He felt her arm encircle his waist and she pressed herself to him so her ripe breast was in his side.

Who needed a siesta anyway?

9

Slocum met her vaqueros in late afternoon when they rode in on their spent horses. Her segundo, Montez, dropped heavily from the saddle and shook Slocum's hand. The last blood rays of sundown shone high on the main house. Horse and rider alike were done in.

"Did you find most of the cattle?" Amanda asked her foreman.

"Some are gone—"

"I understand," she said to him. "Slocum has come to help us."

"It is good. These men do things I can't understand. Why chase our cattle off into the brush?"

"So that you will leave. So that you will quit," Slocum said.

"But this land belongs to the señora and has been in her family for many years."

"Amigo, that is why they want it. The water."

"But we have developed the water for years."

"True. But they want your hard work for the taking."

Montez shook his head and studied the wide-brimmed sombrero in his hands. "I guess we have grown soft since the Comanche is gone."

56

"Yes, we need armed guards and the gates blocked at night. We can't leave the ranch unguarded anymore. The women and children need protection," Slocum said. "They killed your patron. They will kill more if they don't get their way."

"I'm not used to such cruelty," Montez said. "I will be more careful."

"Good. I need a boy to guide me around. I want to learn this country."

Montez nodded. "Pedro, he is a good young man. I will send him to you."

"Good. Was there anything to point to who ran the cattle off?"

"Hoof prints."

"See anything different about them?" Slocum asked.

Montez shook his head. "Nothing, except they were shod horses."

"Good. I need to know anything that you can find out about the ones that ran the cattle off."

"Oh, we found this," he said and dug a paper out of his vest pocket. He handed it to Slocum.

In the half light, Slocum turned it to examine the writing.

Dear Lars,

I have to write and tell you that your father passed away peacefully in his sleep last week. The funeral was very nice. Your brothers were all here. He's been laid to rest in the New Field Cemetery.

Your sister, Sarah Jane Griggs

"A Lars work for Bixby?"

"I don't know."

"Go be with your family. I will keep this," Slocum said to Montez and nodded.

"You hungry?" Amanda asked.

"Sure," he said, realizing she was still there with him in the twilight.

"We will go to the house then," she said. "He has given you the boy Pedro for a guide. He would be my choice, too."

"How old is he?"

"Oh, sixteen, but he is very grown up."

"Good." His arm over her shoulder, they went for the house.

In the early morning, Slocum used his telescope to study Bixby's outfit. Nothing fancy—a rock house with low eaves, some adobe buildings, one that no doubt housed the men. No obvious guards that he could make out. Some Mexican people looked to be busy working around the place as laborers.

Slocum turned to the fresh-faced youth beside him. Hatless so his sombrero couldn't be spotted, he was bellied down beside Slocum.

"Can we catch their saddle horses with the grain we brought?" Slocum asked.

"We can catch several," the youth said with a grin.

"Let's move around there and see how good we are at that."

Bixby's spare horses were ranging north of the place in a trap of mesquites and live oak. Slocum carried a pair of nippers and a punch. He hoped to use them if they could catch some of Bixby's horses. His plans were to try to remove at least one shoe off as many horses in the pasture as possible and hence put Bixby's men afoot. A shod horse ridden barefooted would soon go lame in the rocky hill country.

Pedro found the first ones and his grain lured them in fast so Slocum could pull off the shoes. The youth squatted holding six more horses by leads while Slocum bent over and pried free their shoes. He tried to find the ones that were loose—they came off faster. A pile of shoes began to build. So by noontime he had pulled over forty.

He straightened his weary back and nodded. Pedro ran off the last loose horse and hurried to get their mounts. Slocum used some cedar branches to drag away their tracks. He hid the old shoes in some rock outcroppings, then hurried to where the boy held the saddled horses.

"What next, señor?"

"Tonight, we work on cinches."

"How is that, señor?"

"Do these men go to some cantina?"

"When they have money, they do."

"Good. If any go to town, we will work on their cinches."

"Then what?"

"We will stop their windmills. I want them real busy fixing things."

"I see what you mean." Pedro smiled broadly. "I am glad they sent me with you."

"Just remember, if they ever catch us, they won't treat us nice."

"I savvy nice."

Slocum smiled. They might even jinx a few windmills now, on the ride back. Give them a taste of their own medicine.

He pointed to a mill that was spinning in the strong south wind. When they rode up close to the machinery, they scattered a few spotted longhorns and their calves away from the tank.

"Can you climb up and turn the fan off?" Slocum asked the boy.

"Sure can."

"Be careful," Slocum said and searched around the cedars to be certain they were alone.

The youth went quickly up the ladder and disengaged the drive, and Slocum used a wrench from his saddlebags to undo the bolts on the connecting rod. They pulled the bolts out and let the pump rod drop down so it was barely visible. Then the boy took their horses and Slocum wiped out their tracks around the mill.

"One windmill's not working," Pedro said with a big grin and handed him the reins to his horse.

"There will be more," Slocum said. "If he don't get the clue."

"Plenty of work to reshoe those horses." Pedro laughed aloud, and they loped over the hill for the ranch.

Slocum met Montez at the corrals and the man nodded.

"Let me return these," Slocum said and removed the blacksmith tools sticking out from his saddlebags.

"Sure. What did you do with them?" the man asked, falling in beside him.

"Pulled one or two shoes off each of Bixby's saddle horses."

"Huh?"

"They'll have to reshoe them. Keep them busy. We also shut down a windmill. I want some tough men to shut down some more of his windmills."

"I have some men could do that."

"We won't wreck them this time. But I want them shut down all over. Maybe some just shut off all over his ranch. He doesn't learn a lesson, we will do tougher things to him."

"He will be wary pretty quick and set up guards, won't he?"

"Right, but if he has to have men guarding every windmill, he can't run off your cattle."

Montez smiled with pleasure and bobbed his head. "I like your ways, Slocum."

"We will start easy. Our lessons will increase as needed." He clapped the man on the shoulder.

The foreman agreed. Slocum headed for the house.

Later that evening, Pedro and he planned to ride for the cantina where the Bixby men hung out.

"Ah, you are all right," Amanda said, rushing across the room to hug him. "How was your day?"

"Backbreaking, but I took the shoes off forty horses."

"Why—you are not hired to be a blacksmith?"

He told her his story and she shook her head in dismay. "I could have sent you men to help."

"No, we need to be quiet. He must not see us yet. I only do things now to show him what I can really do to him in return."

"But how will this—"

"He's busy fixing his own things, how can he harm you?"

"Come and eat, it will soon be cold." She dragged him by the arm to the table.

He nodded in approval at the great spread she had prepared for him: a large roast of beef to be carved, dishes of food in red sauce and fresh vegetables from the ranch's garden; tortillas and red wine; the silverware polished until it sparkled under the crystal chandelier's light.

Slocum ate until he could hold no more, then toasted Amanda with his wineglass. "To our winning the war."

"Yes. What will you do next?"

"Oh . . . Pedro and I are going to some cantina and look for his men."

"Tonight?" Disappointment was written on her face.

"Yes, but I will return before the rooster crows."

"Good." She looked around, then lowered her voice. "Come to my room when you do get back."

"I shall." He raised the glass again to her.

They found the cantina when the quarter moon rose. Music came from the inside and the sounds of women's laughter carried on the night air. The place was set in a grove of trees, and the yellow light of Chinese lanterns spread out into the woods, giving long shadows from the trunks.

The cowboys' horses were standing hipshot in a line to the right at hitchracks. Slocum and Pedro slipped in, talking softly and easing their knife blades under the mohair cinches to saw them about in two. One by one they worked over the twenty or so girths, until they were satisfied that at the least strain past climbing aboard, the cinches would give way and dump their riders.

Slocum moved closer and could see several of the gunhands having themselves a real fandango with the Mexican girls in low-cut dresses that they whirled around the floor. Drinking and dancing, they obviously were having a big time. The shrill laughter of the women rung in the night, and waiters rushed about delivering drinks to the halfway insulting rannies.

Slocum tried to find sight of Wilson, but couldn't make him out. He could see the wagon-wheel lamp in the middle of the room hung on a rope from the ceiling. If he could cut that down, the party would be over for a while.

His plan was to shoot up the place to get them to run out and charge after him and Pedro. It might work. He drew the .44-40 out of the scabbard and laid it across the saddle.

"Get on your horse," he said softly to Pedro. "We ride out after this."

He took careful aim and the rifle report shattered the night. The lamp came crashing down and the music stopped. Aside from the screams of the women, the night grew silent.

"Get the hell out of the hill country!" Slocum shouted. "Or you'll all be dead."

He turned Buck and set out after Pedro. A few pistol shots answered him, but he knew if they returned some gunfire from the far side of the woods, the half-drunk, angry rannies would take up chase. So he shoved the rifle in the saddle scabbard and drew his Colt. He gave five quick shots back at the cantina. They answered with more in his direction, but by then he was out of their range.

Men shouted, "Get to your horses and get them bastards!"

Slocum nodded at Pedro and they tore off in the night. From the top of the ridge, they watched the riders in the starlight charge out of the woods and lash their horses. Under the strain, riders and saddles began to fall off their horses. The confusion caused other horses to shy, and their girths gave way, with spilled riders cursing and shouting blue obscenities in the darkness.

"Time we got us some sleep," Slocum said to Pedro and headed Buck northeasterly for Amanda's place. He drew in a deep breath of the pungent cedar aroma that flooded the night air, and laughed. "They're going to learn, Pedro."

"I think so, too."

Both men chuckled as they set their ponies in a long lope for home.

10

"What in the hell are you talking about?" Bixby asked the Mexican wrangler.

"Someone pulled de shoes off the saddle horses."

"You crazy sumbitch, no one pulls the shoes off someone else's saddle horses. What've you been drinking?" Totally put out at the dumb bastard with the sombrero clutched to his chest, he stared out the window at the open dirt yard. No way that someone could sneak up on this ranch and pull the shoes—

"Where are the shoes at?"

"Señor, I have no idea." The wrangler shrugged his shoulders. "Gone. They vamoose like a ghost done it."

"Shit, I don't believe a word of it. You go catch some of them horses and bring them up here. How many are there?" Bixby slapped his hat on and followed the Mexican out the front door.

"Mitch!" he shouted at one of the gunhands walking toward the kitchen.

"Yeah, Boss?"

"Someone's taken the damn shoes off our horses, Juan says."

"In the horse pasture?" Mitch asked, shocked.

"They ain't been nowhere's else. Get someone who can track and we'll see about this deal."

"Sure. Alex can track. I'll get him."

"Don't be all day, either."

"Right." And the gunslinger began to run for the long, low bunkhouse.

How in hell's name could someone get those horses and take off their shoes?

"See your good sorrel, he has only two shoes." Juan pointed at Bixby's favorite horse he had led up to show him.

"They were just put on." Bixby ducked through the corral bars and caught the red horse. He lifted the front hoof and could see how freshly the shoe had been pulled. He swore when he let go of the hoof.

Several of the hands joined him and began searching the ground. Bixby shook his head. "They can pull shoes off our damn horses, they can shoot us as easy, remember that."

"Down here," Alex called and they all hurried over to the wash.

"They used grain to lure them back here," Alex said, pointing at the hulls on the ground.

"How many were there?"

"Two or three."

"Two or three pulled all those shoes off that many horses and we never saw them?"

"They were out of sight back here."

"Everyone can get busy reshoeing them."

"Señor, we don't have that many horseshoes."

"What did they do with them?"

"Stuck them up their ass," Alex said. "I doubt that they left any."

"One of you take a buckboard to town and go buy a keg— make it two kegs of shoes. When you get back—if it takes all night, I want this bunch reshod." He looked over the men.

"Yes, sir," came their reply. Bixby shook his head in

disgust. This new man she hired was behind all this then, because them dumb Messikins never knew to do anything like this before he got there.

Suppertime, Bixby took the meal in his office and was cutting a tough steak when someone burst through the open double doors.

"Señor?"

"What now?" he said, not looking at the flush-faced man in the doorway.

"They have broken the windmills."

"What?" He threw down his napkin and looked at the tin tiles in the ceiling for help. "How many?"

The man shrugged. "Several—I couldn't fix all of them."

Bixby closed his eyes. As soon as they got his red horse reshod, he planned to ride down and find McKlein and see why in the hell he hadn't arrested this Slocum or whoever.

It was past midnight when Bixby rode up to the small wooden bungalow. He dropped heavily from the saddle. His spurs gave a clang and he went through the picket-fence gate. Something was blooming and he thought it might be sweetpea flowers.

"McKlein!" he shouted from the open front door into the dark house.

A boy's voice gave a startled yelp and it was cut off by someone gagging him. "Shut up. It's only Bixby. I'm coming."

"I didn't know," the youth protested.

"Shut up."

Bixby scowled. He never knew McKlein had any boys of his own. Then he saw the sheriff in the doorway. "What in the fuck is going on with you—my horses been crippled and my windmills wrecked by that sumbitch Slocum."

"When?" McKlein asked, buttoning his shirt in the starlight.

"Today, stupid. They got the shoes off my horses and then wrecked my windmills."

"All of them?"

"How should I know? We ain't been to all of them."

"Who do you figure is behind all this?"

"Why, that sumbitch Slocum. No one else ever figured all that out before."

McKlein sighed. "I'll go arrest him."

"If you'd done that in the first place, this would never have happened. It's costing me big money."

"All right, I'll arrest him in the morning."

"Need me to go along?"

"No. I can handle one man by myself."

Bixby wasn't so certain about that even. McKlein hadn't done a damn thing so far. Law or no law, he was getting this Slocum and making an example out of them greasers that they wouldn't ever forget.

11

"The sheriff is here," she whispered in Slocum's ear.

"So soon." He rose up. His eyes filled with grit and he tried to focus them on her concerned face. Light filtered into the room. "What's he want?"

"Says he has a warrant for your arrest for murdering Cave Bixby."

Slocum blinked. "From whom?"

She shrugged. "I have no idea."

"I do." He threw his legs out of the bed. "It's an excuse to take me in and shoot me in the back on the way, saying that I tried to escape."

"What can we do?"

"I'll read the warrant first."

"But—"

"He have a posse?"

"No, he came alone."

"Good. He figured I would not go with him and would run off. Then he'd have an excuse to run me down, right?"

"I don't know how such men think." She looked upset. "What can I do?"

"Stand back." He pulled on his pants, then socks and boots. He put on a fresh white shirt she handed him and buttoned it up the front, then knifed it into his pants with the flat of his hands. The six-gun strapped on, he nodded for her to go ahead.

She looked questioningly at him, then obeyed.

Slocum saw the man as he looked up at him with his squinted right eye holding the gaze. "Sheriff Talbot McKlein. I have a warrant for your arrest."

"Let me see it," Slocum said and took the paper to study it.

"It's filed in this county," Slocum said, looking over at the man.

"It's valid. Signed by Judge Norstrum himself."

Slocum shook his head. "This Cave Bixby was not shot in this county. No way you can file a felony warrant in another county than where the alleged crime occurred."

"I have his body and he was shot three times in the back. That's murder."

"McKlein, even in a crooked court of law that won't work."

"You some kinda damn lawyer?"

"I know the law. This paper is worthless and I'm not surrendering to this piece of crap."

McKlein went for his gun butt, but Slocum pulled his own out first. The lawman blinked in disbelief at the muzzle pointed at him. He let go and his pistol fell back in the holster. "I'll have you know I'm law in this county—"

"Bixby's law, huh? You never brought in a killer for her husband. You've never stopped the raids on her cattle and neighbors. That, sir, is malfeasance of office and the Texas Rangers are on their way right now to check all that out."

"I'm the law here! You've drawn on the—"

"Unbuckle your gunbelt and drop it. I'm tired of your mouth. Law is one thing. Hiding behind the badge to enforce criminal actions will get you twenty years under Texas law. And believe me, I know judges that will give you more than that. We'll see how tough you are when the Rangers get here."

"There ain't no Rangers coming here—"

"Why? Because you bribed off the first one they sent?" McKlein blinked his eyes and frowned. "Hell—no."

Slocum knew the truth, despite the lawman's denial. Somehow McKlein had stopped the Rangers from coming, and that was why Amanda had never seen them. It would be different the next time they sent them.

"Now turn around and march for your horse," Slocum ordered.

"You won't get by with this. I swear you'll be in my jail or the funeral home in less than twenty-four hours."

"Funeral home—that's where you want me, right?" He gave the man a shove toward the front door. "Bring the sheriff's gun," he said to Amanda as he marched him out to his horse.

He holstered his own, removed the bullets from Mc-Klein's weapon and shoved the holster set at him.

"Get on your horse and go tell Bixby that his bluff never worked. Tell the Colonel he has only seen the start of his troubles if he don't come and ask for peace."

"He'll never do that."

"Well, then his stubbornness will get him hurt. We don't intend to stand by and let him harass any more of the Mexican or any other ranchers in this country. We can cure a dog of sucking eggs. We can cure him, too."

"I'll have you in jail—"

Slocum swung around and kicked McKlein's horse in the gut. The gelding shied and about unseated the lawman. "Get the hell off this ranch and stay off. Start counting your free days now. You'll do a stretch behind them bars yourself and it won't be long starting."

His horse at last under control, McKlein glared at Slocum, his lips so tight they looked ready to bust. Then he swung the horse around and left.

"Send for Pedro," Slocum said to Amanda. "I'm writing a letter to Captain Rob in San Antonio. Pedro can take it to him personally. Rob'll send help this time that will end this business with Bixby and his law dog that he sent to bite me."

"You think—" She hesitated. "I've sent three telegrams."

"They must have headed them off." Slocum glared westward long after the lawman in the black suit was out of sight.

She swung on his arm. "Come and eat some breakfast. You are acting too mad."

"I'll be mad from here on."

Out of breath, Pedro came with his sombrero in his hand to report to him.

"Have you ever been to San Antonio?" he asked the youth.

"*Sí*, I have driven cattle there."

"Good. I am sending a letter with you to Captain Rob of the Texas Rangers. No one must see it but him. Not any of the other Rangers or anyone. If Bixby learns of your business, he will send men to stop you. McKlein would do the same. I have a friend in San Antonio you can trust. His name is Tony Petillio. He owns the Oasis Verde Restaurant on the south side of the Alamo Square."

Pedro nodded and accepted the envelope. "Captain Rob only?"

"He's the only one to give that to," Slocum warned him. "Then find Tony. He will protect you."

"Here is money for the trip," Amanda said, giving him a purse. "Be very careful, Pedro. Your mother needs you."

"*Sí, señora,* I will be careful. When should I leave?"

"Dark," Slocum said. "So you can go by town undercover and ride wide around it before you get back on the road."

"After I give this to Captain Rob?"

"He will no doubt have a message for you to bring back, after you get some rest." Slocum handed the youth the .30-caliber pistol in a small holster. "If you have to save your life, use this."

"*Sí.*" The youth swallowed hard and nodded as he accepted it.

"Take one of my best horses to ride there," Amanda said.

Lights danced with excitement in Pedro's eyes. *"Sí, señora."*

"Most of all you must deliver the message," Slocum said.

"I will. I swear upon my life I will."

Slocum rose and clapped him on the shoulder. "I know you will."

The youth left. Slocum hugged Amanda while they were alone in the room. "Now the war has begun, we must finish it."

"How?"

"I think he will have guards at the windmills from now on. One or two and we will slip up, take them. Then undress them and shear their heads, so we can tell them. Give them twenty-four hours to leave the country or else."

"But—"

He kissed her hard on the mouth. "Don't worry. Montez and I are going out today and start our sheep shearing business."

"Oh, Slocum . . . I don't know—"

"It will work," he promised her and kissed her sweet mouth again, leaving her breathless.

"We have the shears, señor," Montez reported. With him were two more vaqueros, Bigoata and Rafael, both men in their thirties, wearing the dress of their ancestors—ponchos, for the wind was cooler that day, and sombreros—and carrying six-guns and knives. Montez swore they were his best fighters.

They squatted beside the corral, their backs to the sharp wind, and Slocum explained his plan. They would sneak up on the guards that Bixby had posted at the windmills, jump them, shear off their hair and let them ride back to Bixby's ranch naked.

"I don't want them killed. But if they fight, they can die, too."

The two men looked at each other and laughed.

"It will be very cold to ride home without your clothes," Bigoata said and chuckled with his partner.

"Ride out of this country," Slocum said. "They don't leave, they're marked men. Bald heads. They'll have gotten their only warning."

The men nodded that they understood. The four mounted up and headed for where Montez figured that Bixby would post the first of his guards.

From a ridge, Slocum eyed the windmill with his telescope. At first he could see nothing, but then a wisp of smoke gave away the lookout.

"They've built a fire to keep warm," he said and handed the glass to Montez bellied down beside him.

"I can't believe that," Montez said, handing back the glass.

"These are not the toughest gunfighters, or the smartest," Slocum said, and they headed for their horses. Montez felt they could ride in closer, before going on foot the last part.

A half hour later, Slocum could smell the smoke and hear the men's voices from where he rested in a dry wash. The other three were working in from the far side. He drew his gun and scaled the side of the wash. He went in a low crawl toward the cedars that separated him from the guards. Wind in the evergreen bows covered most of the sounds they would make approaching the two.

"Hands in the air!" someone shouted.

Slocum was on his feet and around the cedar. Both guards had their hands up. Bigoata held his pistol on them and Montez was disarming them. Rafael brought in their horses.

"Start undressing," Slocum said and he nodded in approval when Rafael removed their rifles, then checked their saddlebags for more weapons.

"Undressing?" asked the black bearded one in disbelief.

"Get your clothes off," Slocum ordered.

"What you going to do to us?"

"Get undressed or we'll undress you, and we ain't easy."

"What you going to do with us?"

"We're going to strip you bare naked, shear your hair off and then give you a horse to ride out of this country on. We ever see you anywhere near here again, we'll shoot you like a damn dog."

"Hell," the tall one swallowed hard, "I'd get the hell out of this country in my clothes and never come back."

"Naw, you'd go running to Bixby and be right back running off these folks' cattle. Get undressed and then sit on the ground. You've got a haircut coming."

"Sonsabitches—"

Slocum stepped over and jerked open the bearded one's shirt, jammed it off his shoulder and drew him up close with a fist full of his underwear. "Listen real good. You want to fill a buzzard's gut, you keep talking big. I have no reason not to kill you right here and now."

"All right." The man hurriedly shed his clothing, and Rafael stepped in and began clipping the tall one's hair. He winced a few times but sat on the ground huddled up, hugging his arms about him and shivering in the wind. The haircut complete, the bearded one knelt down and Rafael started for him.

Slocum held him back for a second and pressed the muzzle of his Colt to the gunman's skull. "You try anything, you're dead. Hear me?"

"Yeah."

He nodded for Rafael to start. The vaquero also clipped lots of the beard away. He stepped back when he'd finished, to admire his work.

"Get on your horses. We better not see you in this country again. If you show your faces around here again, you better have a good suit to wear for your funeral."

"I won't ever forget you for this," the bearded one said, looking like a pale ghost in the saddle. Both men's white skin shone like bleached sheets in the sunlight. Their heads showing the choppy haircuts, they booted their horses away.

"Good job," Slocum said as Bigoata came down from shutting off the mill. Bixby would have to send someone else back to turn it on. "Let's ride. We need to find at least two more sets."

One gunman guarded the next mill. They tied him up to shear him and finally stuck the squawking, naked gunfighter on his horse and sent him packing. They laughed for a few minutes at his indignation over their handling, before they rode on for number three.

The next guards were cooking supper when they got the drop on them. Their boiled beans with fat pork and coffee tasted good to Slocum and his crew after they'd undressed and sheared them, and sent the naked cowhands off in the growing darkness on horseback.

"That makes seven we've run off. How many hands he got?" Slocum asked.

"He had close to thirty at one time," Montez said. "Couple's crippled up. Said they had broke arms and legs from falling off their horses chasing you and Pedro in the night. Doc told someone there were several bunged up over that."

"Two got their ears notched in San Antonio. They won't be back."

"Ears notched?" Bigoata asked.

"Two of them were following the señora around. Couple of guys convinced them to leave this part of the country. Guess they were poor learners—so they notched their ears."

"Whew, we are easy, only cutting their hair."

"All they need is a message. This time," Slocum added as they rode in the dark for the ranch.

"Maybe he will get desperate and raid the ranch?" Montez asked.

"He may, but the word gets out about what's happened to his men, he'll have hell hiring any more."

"I heard he still didn't have all his horses reshod," Montez said with a laugh as a coyote began to wail on the ridge.

Slocum felt good and laughed with them over the horseshoe deal. "As much work as that was, I hope it caused him all kinds of grief." But his mind was on the warm bed and the lovely body that waited for him as he huddled in his jumper against the night wind. Be teeth-chattering cold to be out there with only a yellow slicker from behind your saddle to wear, like those gunnies they'd sheared.

Them boys they fixed that day better have learned all they wanted to know about this range war business.

12

All Bixby needed was more bad news. By this time, Mc-Klein must have back shot that damn Slocum and brought his body into town. It would be no problem to run off them Messikins without him. He'd promised that ranch house to McKlein, and trying to keep that plum from being destroyed had been the thing holding him back. His boys got too rambunctious and they'd burn her down. Damn, this wasn't a war like the last one—and he needed McKlein to cover his ass.

Damn near sundown, he put the pen away and rose from behind the desk. Who was out there naked in the yard? He watched them through the window. Damn, who was their barber? Hatless, they looked clipped, showing their heads to some of the other hands. What was going on? He could hear some of them laughing at the sheared ones' plight.

A big Texas cowboy wearing a towel crossed the yard. "I want my pay. I'm quitting."

"What the hell happened to you today? You're supposed to be guarding a mill. What're you doing back here?"

"I got a gun stuck up my ass by a white guy and three greasers. They sheared us, stripped us naked and then disassembled the windmill. Give me my money."

"A couple of wetbacks jump you and you're running away?"

"Wetbacks, hell, they was toughs and I ain't too sure they wasn't the same ones notched old Taker and Nichols in San Anton. My money please." He held out his calloused palm for it.

"What did they tell you?"

"If we didn't leave the country, they was cutting our balls off and notching us next time they caught us. Said that's why they sheared us, so they'd know who they'd warned."

"Bullshit! They can't—"

"Pay me, Bixby. I ain't going to be here for it."

"I've got a howitzer ready that will send them on the run pissing in their pants."

"Listen, I ain't pissing in mine again. Pay me."

He paid off five hands that evening. Didn't need them anyhow. He hoped he had the parts to repair the mills. He'd send some real guards out in the morning.

A windy morning the next day, he crossed the yard into the face of it. He looked up and saw two riders in the dust. No, three. They weren't his crew—then he noticed the badges on two of them. McKlein's men. Who did they have with them? Slocum? No, it was some boy.

Bixby held his hat on and walked sideways into the blast to meet them.

"Who's he?" Bixby asked over the wind's howl. Their prisoner had been shot, lots of blood on his shirt.

"A Debaca hand named Pedro. Had a letter for some Ranger. McKlein figured you wanted him."

"He arrest Slocum yet?"

"No. He had some problems about jurisdiction."

Bixby nodded. More damn poor excuses was all it was. "Take him to that shed over there. I'll get some men to watch him. He may tell us all we need to know."

The deputy agreed and jerked the youth off the horse.

They headed for the shed. Bixby went to the bunkhouse to see who he had in reserve.

"Dun, you set up a guard detail. We've got a new prisoner in the shed. Do it army style and don't let him get away."

"I can handle it." Dun called to another to help him and then took off on the double.

The kid bound to a chair wouldn't tell them much when Bixby tried to interrogate him. He finally fainted, and two buckets of water did not revive him. Bixby left a man in charge of the shed about sundown and went to the house. More than anything he needed a drink.

In the morning the kid would talk. They'd get tough on him if he didn't spill the beans about Slocum's plans. Bixby's mind was on the girl Edora. He'd ordered her to take a bath and wear a blouse and skirt he'd found for her. She was to entertain him that evening. All this business about the horses, windmill raids and shearing his men's heads—he had about forgot about more basic things like what was between his legs. This night he would serve her on a platter to his dick.

The wine flowed and he made her drink it, then dance for him, while an old woman played a guitar. She whirled dreamlike on the tiles around the room.

"Take off your blouse," he said, anxious to see her firm breasts move with her steps.

When she hesitated, he waved his hand at her to hurry. "Undelay!"

Soon she stepped to the music, and her pointed breasts shook with her every move in the half light of his room. One day, the Debaca woman would do this for him. Damn, he could hardly wait. He had expected her to be his long ago. Ever since he paid McKlein the money for the back-shooter who killed her husband. He did that job right anyway.

"Now the skirt, my pretty one."

She nodded that she heard him and began to untie the strings at her waist. The garment slipped away and he watched her beautiful legs leap and twist. Her tight ass reflected the candle's light . . .

Filled with a big need for her body, he rose and went to her. He swept her in his arms like he would the Debaca woman.

"Keep playing," he said to the old woman. It would be bombs away when he sent his cannon up there. That Slocum would wish he'd never accepted the job with her. He shed his pants and climbed on Edora as he would someday climb on that Debaca bitch's ass.

"Here," he grunted and shoved his big sword into her.

13

They rode in after midnight, calling out to the guard before they entered the gate.

"Come on in. Slocum, you better check on things. An hour ago, the señora's gray horse returned with no rider," the guard told them, standing on the wall in the starlight, with a rifle in the crook of his arm.

"The one Pedro rode out on?" Slocum asked.

"Sí, señor."

Slocum only had a few seconds to consider the latest problem. Had they shot Pedro? Damn their no-good hides—

"Oh, thank God, you're back," Amanda exclaimed, rushing from the main house with a candle lamp to join him. "He tell you about poor Pedro? There's blood on the saddle, too."

Slocum dropped his weary frame from the horse, pulled his pant legs down to free his crotch and shook his head. They were waiting for Pedro, lying in wait somewhere out there. McKlein could not take a chance on anyone getting word to the Rangers. Not from her place at least. Bixby'd bought himself more time, hoping that if he could destroy her and the ranch, the whole thing would blow over and could be covered up. All of Slocum's moves earlier had only made a chained dog all the more vicious. And while he might stop Bixby by stripping his men and sending them packing, McKlein had even more to lose—enough to kill over.

Pedro's mother was crying. He could hear her in the background as Montez and the others gathered around him beside the corral.

"Get me a fresh horse. I'll go get the Rangers," Slocum said, filled with a new determination to stop this range war business. But his greatest concern was for the safety and recovery of the young man.

"You can't," Amanda cried. "We need you here." She handed aside the lamp and tackled him. "I lost one man to them. Not you, too, Slocum."

He hugged her and patted her on the back. "I better go."

"I can go to San Antonio," Rafael said. "I know the back ways."

"They may be guarding them, too," Slocum said.

"Give me two pistols and I will make it."

"You'll need saddle holsters for them, so they're hooked on the horn for your quick use."

"Sí," Rafael said.

"I'm going to the house and write the letter," Slocum said. "Go get some food and supplies, too. I'll have it written in a few minutes."

"Take a good horse of mine," Amanda said, "and be careful."

"I will, señora."

"I know where such a holster is," Montez said and hurried off.

In no time, Rafael rode out the back way from the ranch, planning to skirt north this time for San Antonio. Slocum wished him luck, then checked with both wall guards. No sign of anything. The gates were blocked with wagons and he felt secure enough, so he went back and joined Amanda.

"You are upset," she said, joining him as he swept into the house.

"I have these gut feelings and I can't help them. Something is going on out there and I can't put a finger on it. I should ride to Bixby's and see if Pedro is a prisoner of theirs."

"But it is late and you've had no sleep."

"Things are happening fast in this deal." He couldn't clear his mind of his need to go and see about Pedro, alive or dead. He was uncertain. Maybe they would hold him as a hostage. Damn, he had to know what happened to the youth. And if he found out who had done this—he planned to personally kick their ass up to their shoulders.

He caught her by both arms and kissed her hard. When they tore their faces apart, he wet his lips, tasting the honey on them. "I must go try to find Pedro. If he's alive I may be able to save him."

"But it's so late."

"Maybe not too late for him."

"Can I go?"

He shook his head. "I'd love to have you with me, but this isn't the time or the place. I must go alone."

"Do what you must then. But please, Slocum, be careful?"

"I will. Let's have some food and I'll go."

She surrendered and led him to the kitchen. There, she served him some cold chicken and warm beans wrapped in a tortilla, plus fresh hot coffee. Then she went after something. In minutes she returned with a tightly woven wool vest. The quality was superior. The brown stripes in the off-white bands made the garment look dressy.

"To keep you warm. He would have wanted you to wear it."

He slipped into it and buttoned it with the silver conchas. "Very nice."

She pressed it down with her hands and tears appeared in her eyes. "Come back to me, Slocum, please?"

"I will, Amanda."

The ride to Bixby's required a couple of hours. He shortened it and was there in an hour and a half. He left her bay tied out of sight in the wash, then made his way to the bunkhouses. A light in one window told him something must be in there. For any light to be on at this hour of the night was a giveaway.

Careful to stay in the shadows, he moved in that direction until he could ease up and peek in from the side at the room's contents. Saw nothing. Ducked down and then looked back. Whoever was guarding in there was asleep in a chair with a shotgun across his lap. Then when Slocum peered again in the dirty smudged window, he could see Pedro slumped over in the back, bound to a chair. Slocum wondered where he was wounded. No telling. He needed to open the latch, slip inside and batter that guard over the head, so he could get Pedro out of there. The latch string would not work—felt stuck on the inside. He dared not do anything to awaken the guard, who could spread the alarm.

Damn, Bixby and the sheriff had to be in cahoots. They could all rot in jail for what he cared about. Still, in court, things would be hard to prove without witnesses or someone to give testimony. Maybe the Ranger that Rob would send up here would have some ideas. He hoped he would send more than one, but usually it was one trouble, one Ranger. McKlein had no doubt been blocking Amanda's telegrams or a Ranger would have been there already.

He pulled gently on the string again. Nothing. Must be latched inside. It was not going to unlock for him. If he used his foot to smash it open, he'd have to go in guns blazing and that would wake up the whole camp. He wanted a bigger gap between him and the ones that would chase him.

Maybe he'd better check on the horses they had saddled—if they had any. In the pens, he found a half dozen snoring, asleep on their feet. He unhitched them and led them out of the corral. Quickly, he stripped off the saddles and bridles, then sent the ponies out the gate for the pasture. Good. That would slow any pursuit.

Being cautious, he saw, then heard the figure come out of the bunkhouse, coughing away. Close—if he had come outside a few minutes sooner, he might have caught Slocum heading off the horses. Pressed to the corral and squatted down on his heels, Slocum watched the silhouette of the individual headed for the lighted window.

Maybe changing the guard. Slocum moved to a parked wagon, slipped under it and soon was back in the shadows of the bunkhouse porch and fifty feet behind the one headed for the door.

Two raps and the guard inside demanded to know who it was.

"Kerby Jones."

Slocum sucked himself against the wall. Jones looked around, then stepped inside the doorway. They left the door open for some reason. Slocum undid the strap over the hammer of his Colt and hurried to get beside the structure, ducking his head, for the rafters were lower than the porch.

"About time you got here," someone grumbled.

"Yeah, you would have slept the damn night away."

"You hear any more about them guys that them greasers jumped?"

"No, Twister came in about dark, said he'd seen Kurt wearing a raincoat and scared shitless."

"How's that?"

"They sheared his fucking head, took all his clothes and told him they'd cut off his balls next time if he didn't quit the country."

"Holy Jesus. Who else did they do that to?"

"Must have been a half dozen or more. They ain't no sign of Blacky and that lanky Texan, Earl."

"Blacky was tough."

"Yeah, but them Mexicans are tougher when they want to be."

"You figuring on staying on then?"

"Hey, he only pays ten bucks over cowboy wages for this job. That Mexican dies over there and we can all hang."

"Aw, he'll hide his body, won't he?"

"Maybe."

"I've got a better idea." Slocum stepped inside and pointed his six-gun at them. "Start undressing."

"Oh, hell—"

The two made faces, but they obeyed him.

"What the hell we doing this for?" the balding one asked.

"So you will remember that the next time I catch you, I'll geld you."

"You sumbitch—"

Slocum busted him over the head with the butt of his gun. "Now you finish getting undressed," he said to the other one as the first gunman lay crumbled to the floor.

"I'm stripping. I'm hurrying." With shaky hands, he shed his clothing and soon stood like a white fence post.

Slocum had gone to check on Pedro. He slipped behind the youth to cut the ropes securing him to the chair.

"Can you hear me, Pedro?"

"Sí, señor."

"Good, I'll get you untied. Do you think you can walk to my horse?"

"I will try."

Slocum doubted the boy could do much walking. "I'll tie these two up and then we'll go to the horse."

"Fine," Pedro agreed, rubbing his wrists.

"Where did they shoot you?"

"It was only a scratch." He lifted his shirt to show the place on his side.

.

"You must have lost some blood. The saddle had plenty on it."

Pedro forced a smile. "I knew he would go home."

"He did." Slocum tied up the unconscious cowboy then motioned for the naked one to sit in the chair. He quickly tied his hands behind his back and stuffed a rag in his mouth.

Then he made a gag for the moaning one on the floor and stuffed it in his mouth. That silenced his groaning.

He told Pedro to throw his arm over his shoulder so he could support him, and they headed out the door into the night. Their gait was slow, but soon they were out in the starlight, headed for the dark cedars, and the itching on the back of Slocum's neck let up. He loaded the youth into the saddle, then led the horse down the wash. When they came to where the wash entered a wider one, he stepped up in the saddle behind Pedro.

"You making it?"

Pedro nodded with both hands wrapped around the saddle horn, and Slocum hoped the boy didn't faint. Someone needed to get through to the Rangers. He hoped that Rafael was on his way. The Bixby hands would be harder to get the jump on after the things done to them over the past few days. Still, him and her men's efforts must have put the fear of God into some of them.

"You making it?" he asked the youth.

"Trying, Slocum, trying."

14

As day broke over his shoulder, he smiled at the rooster's loud crowing. He wondered if the swaying youth in the saddle in front of him had even heard the cockerel greeting the morning.

"You still there?" he asked, reining the horse toward the main gate.

Pedro mumbled; he'd make it.

"Señor Slocum—oh, you have Pedro!" the guard on the gate shouted. "I'll move the *carreta* for you." He disappeared from view and soon the cart was pulled aside.

"Thanks," Slocum said and headed the horse in. Weary as his riders, the gelding snorted loudly in the dust and raised his head, entering the compound to the bark of dogs and cheering of the children to welcome them. Slocum nodded and dropped heavily to the ground. He reached up and helped the blanch-faced youth to dismount.

"How is he?" a woman asked from behind his back.

"Doing good. His wound does not look to be too serious." He held Pedro up as he tried to make his sea legs work.

"We can take him," Montez said. The foreman and another stepped in and supported the youth.

88

"Who did this to you?" Montez demanded.

"Bixby's men. They got your letter, too," he said to Slocum.

"It's okay. Another man has gone for the Rangers."

"I'm sorry—" Then his knees buckled and several women sucked in their breath.

"Get him in bed and check his wound," Slocum said. "The ride may have worn him out."

Satisfied that enough people were seeing about Pedro's welfare, he headed for the house. His eyes felt like sand pits and his mind was clogged with all he knew about the enemy. Bixby had a dedicated effort out to stop any messages getting out of the area. That meant that he and Mc-Klein were in cahoots like Slocum suspected—Amanda's accusation in the first place.

"Morning," he said to the women in the kitchen, busy preparing food and shocked to see him.

"Pedro's all right. A little worse for wear, but he'll be fine."

He saw a dark-haired teenager cross herself and then nod to him in approval. A cute one, no doubt more than flirtation there, for she looked very sincere over Pedro's safety.

"How is the food?" Slocum asked.

"We can serve you in the dining room," the woman in charge said.

"I can eat right here. What can we eat?"

She smiled at him. "We have coffee?"

"Fine, pour me some," he said and held out a fresh cup for the woman with the pot to fill.

"We have eggs, frijoles and some *carrizo*," the boss one said, sweeping her hair from her face with the back side of her hand. "Take a seat," she said, holding a straight-backed chair for him to sit at the side of the great table covered in produce from the garden and red meat being cut into chunks for some dish they would prepare.

"We are supposed to awaken the *patrone* when you got back."

"Let her sleep and you can tell me all the gossip while I eat."

His words drew a snicker from the younger helpers. The boss shook her head as if to scold him and ended laughing aloud with the others.

"Well, what is the gossip this morning?" He sat up in the chair as if ready to hear anything.

"Tina is going to have a baby."

The girl took a step from the group and gave a bow. Hardly showing anything at this stage, she looked pleased over her condition, though the whole thing had brought a blush to her face.

"Boy or girl?" he asked between sips of the hot coffee.

Unable to speak, she shrugged at him.

"So it is healthy," he said to ease her misery.

"A certain hombre is cheating on his wife."

"Oh." Then he nodded as if taking it in.

"But we won't tell you his name," the boss said.

"So!" Amanda said from the doorway. "You would let me sleep all day to let all of you flirt with him?"

"Oh, no." He twisted to smile at her.

"Well, did you find Pedro?"

"Yes. He's at his mother's house and I'm sure he will live."

"Wonderful!" She hugged his neck and then she smiled at the girl with a platter of food she delivered to him. "So you plan to fatten him, too."

Everyone laughed. Amanda ordered herself breakfast and took the steaming coffee cup from the hand of the girl. She pulled up a chair beside him.

"You look very tired."

"I could sleep, but fear that I need to do more to upset Bixby's men."

"You better sleep a few hours first."

"Rafael should get there with luck by tonight."

"I am certain he has gotten past their lookouts by now."

He nodded and hoped she was right.

"What's that noise?" he asked at the first boom. "Sounds like a cannon." He threw down the napkin from his lap and hurried out the back door. Blinking his eyes against the bright sun, he shouted at the guard on the wall in front. "What's going on?"

"They have a cannon, señor." The guard pointed to the edges of the cedars.

Holy shit, he had never figured on a cannon. Where did Bixby get one of those? The army. Another boom from an explosion shook the ground under Slocum's boots and he raced to the front wall. He reached the scaffold the guards used and scrambled up to look for the gun. His arrival was in time to see another round come in and explode a hundred feet short of the wall. It blew apart a good-size cedar bush and threw boughs and dirt into the air around the place where it hit.

"Got an old Sharp's rifle?" he asked Amanda as she and the others hurried to peer at the attackers.

"Coming," she said and spun around to head for the house.

"Will they blast us next?" Montez asked from the ground.

"They might if they find their range. Better get the women and children back further," Slocum said, coming off the wall.

"I will. Everyone! They might soon lob a grenade in here and kill many of you. Women and children go to the stables and stay there until this is over. Now!" Montez ordered, using his arms to herd them back.

Amanda approached out of breath, and obviously the weight of the buffalo gun was heavy enough to slow her down. Slocum took the rifle with a thanks, let down the lever and took a cartridge from her.

"What are you going to do?"

"Keep low. We're going to knock out their gunner."

Her shoulders sagged and she dropped her head as if lost in the hopelessness of their situation. Slocum had no time to plead his case. The rifle resting on the wall, he pulled back the first trigger so the lighter last one was ready. Then he looked through the haze and smoke at the man ready to torch off the cannon. He watched him light the fuse on the barrel of the gun.

"Down," he shouted and ducked under the wall.

The whizzing sound first, then the boom of the blast. It struck ten yards from the front gate. The explosion rained down debris on him and the other guard on the stand. Quickly Slocum centered the sights on the X where the gunner's galluses crossed the middle of his back. The main man was busy giving orders to the crew. The rifle lurched into Slocum's shoulder and smoke came from the muzzle long after the projectile left it.

The huge sphere of lead struck the gunner hard in the back and sent him ass over teakettle. He didn't get up either.

Then a younger one tried to get the gun crew to come back and went to waving and giving orders. Slocum shook his head and held out his hand for another round from her. He reloaded, set the first trigger and grimaced at the target. Nothing else to do—he needed to break their will to fire that old gun or the whole ranch crew and their families would be shelled to death before the sun went down.

The Sharp's gave its lusty report and everyone held their pained ears looking downstream. Then the gunner disappeared. Slocum ejected the shell and looked back at the cannon. No one was near it.

"Get four horses saddled and we'll go recover it," he shouted to Montez.

"The cannon?" the man asked in disbelief.

Slocum nodded. "They can't use what they ain't got."

"But—" Amanda started to protest and then silenced herself with her fist pressed to her mouth.

"I need the best shot in the place up here," Slocum said, looking over the crew.

A tough-faced part-Indian came forward. There was no need to quiz this man's skill, for his eyes told Slocum enough. The powerful Sharp's was no stranger to this one. He handed the rifle to him.

"We're going after that cannon. Shoot anyone that you can who tries to stop us."

The Indian's coal black eyes were deep set. He took the rifle and then bent over to get a cartridge from the señora's hand. "I will do that," he said and nodded at Slocum before he climbed off the staging.

A horse was brought up for Slocum. The cart was moved aside from the opening. "Use your pistols when you need to," Slocum said to the other riders and bounded onto the back of the bay horse. In a flash, they were on the run for their goal. Riding four abreast, they charged the hill where the unattended artillery piece sat.

Two men on horseback busted out of the live oaks, shooting at them, but the ranch sharpshooter's bullets cut them down. Slocum reined up the bay at the big gun and booted his horse around in a circle to keep a close eye on the cedars for any more snipers or resistance. Both cannoneers lay facedown in the dirt with bloody backs from the .50-caliber. Lariats were quickly tied on the tongue, dallies taken, and the three charged off with the gun trailing after them. Slocum emptied his handgun at the brush and then set heels to the bay.

A few sporadic shots were all the defense the rest of the gun crew offered as the ranch crew rushed back for the compound. Out of control, the wildly bouncing cannon rolled over three times before they reached the gate. With a roar, a half dozen men rushed out to secure it back on its wheels and guided it inside the gate. Their victory cries warmed Slocum as he looked back over his shoulder and saw no pursuit.

He stepped off his bay before the pony had hardly stopped, and turned his head when the .50-caliber went off on the wall above him. He looked in time to see a rider in the distance pitched off his horse. The mount tucked his tail to his ass and doubled his stride to get away, busting into the cedars.

"Anyone recognize that one?" Slocum asked.

"One they called Thurman," someone said.

"Five down. They're going to need some recruits if my guess is right," he said out loud, patting the hot cannon like a pet animal. "One thing's for certain, they'll have hell using this on us again."

A cheer went up and he nodded, pleased. "It ain't over yet, boys. Bixby is an old war horse, and they never know when to quit."

Sobered by his words, everyone nodded.

"To celebrate tonight, we'll have a fandango," Amanda said to them and hugged Slocum's arm.

"Yes," he said in approval and noticed the white-faced Pedro standing on the porch of his mother's jacal—smiling in approval at him.

"Get some rest," he shouted at the youth.

Pedro nodded he heard his words, then turned to talk to the others gathering around him to hear of his adventure and wounds.

Slocum headed for the house, grateful he could eat some food, then sleep for the next few hours. Amanda hung tight to his arm as if he might escape her—or even wanted to.

What would Bixby try the next time?

15

"They captured the cannon?" Bixby inhaled up his nose. "What about Younkers and Meeker?"

"Dead. Shot them at long range. They must of had a fifty-caliber buffalo gun. They blowed holes in them like outdoors."

"I thought . . ." Bixby collapsed against the wall of the house. How could a cannon fail against simple, dumb Messikins? Oh, damn. There were more problems, too. Between windmill wrecks, the damn hair shearing and the wounded ones—he had four men still laid up from that cantina girth cutting. He should have gone along and been in command. He figured that those two, Younkers and Meeker, would fire a few rounds and them Messikins would scatter like sheep. Instead they opened with deadly sniper fire and took the cannon. One thing, they didn't have many charges for it—cause he didn't either. Of course, if they knew anything at all about cannons, they'd know a few kegs of black powder would do the same thing.

His fist clenched so tight his fingernails bit into his palms, and he suppressed a scream. What would he do next? She would never beat him. He was going to run her and that whole bunch of greasers out of that country up there.

You may have that cannon, Slocum, you bastard, but I'll get you and her, too.

16

She stood by the drapes and looked at the sunset from the bedroom window. The orange light of sundown fired the wall across the room. Still half-asleep, he scrubbed his face in his palms and wondered how long he could have slept—without the need to get up and learn all he could about the day's activities.

"Montez says he thinks that Bixby has sent for more gunmen."

"Where—the border or San Antonio?"

"I think he would hire gringos, bad as he speaks of Mexicans."

"Well, good, he won't find many tough white men there."

"Where are the tough ones?"

"Up in the Indian Nation or Arizona."

"Why there?" she asked.

"The Hashknife has most of the Texas toughs hired to work on their holdings in northern Arizona. They're trying to hold on up there against the Mormons and small ranchers stealing them blind. The rest of the real bad ones are hiding out up in the Indian Nation 'cause they ain't bothered much by anything but a handful of deputy U.S. marshals out of Fort Smith and Judge Issac Parker's court."

She crossed the room and swept back her robe. "Do you have time for me?"

He gazed like a starved man at her firm, pointed breasts and smiled as the robe slid from her shoulders. A mild head shake to make him awake enough to realize this was really happening, and he drew a deep breath and reached out to pull her to him. His mouth sought her smooth skin and raised up in time to capture the quarter-size right nipple in his lips and suckle it as she let out an exhale of pleasure.

Her fingers threaded through the hair above his ears, and she cried out when he changed nipples to the other one. In seconds she was sprawled beside him and their mouths sought to put out the fire consuming them. Pierced by his great erection, she shouted aloud and hunched her back toward his effort to give her all he had to give. When at last he reached the bottom of her shaft, she tossed her head from side to side and moaned.

When he knew any second he would explode, he pressed deep and she clung to him in desperation. Then like a cannon's blast he shot off his gun and a cry escaped her mouth. For a long while, they remained hard pressed, suspended in their desire's red-hot ashes. Until at last they collapsed like an avalanche into the goose-down mattress.

Spent, they napped in each other's arms, and never awoke until starlight fell through the window, to the floor. In the hills to the west, a coyote yapped at the quarter moon rising slow-like out of the east, as if he could hasten its speed. Slocum smiled at the coyote's efforts and washed at the pitcher and bowl on the nightstand. He considered his beard stubble and decided that it would have to wait until later when he had some hot water to scrape it off.

She took him from behind and pressed her ripe body against his back. "You running away?"

"Nope, but you know that someday—I'll have to ride on. I hope that I can stay long enough to get rid of Bixby for you."

"Listen, they've started the music already," she said, not answering him. She ran to the window and looked across the grounds. Someone was lighting the Chinese lanterns, and she snuggled in his arms when he wrapped them around her. The heat from their lovemaking and sleeping so tight was evaporating from her skin.

"You will dance with me?" She looked up for his answer.

"Yes—but the days I can stay here grow shorter."

She twisted around so her breasts stabbed him. Her dark eyes looked up at him. "Yes. But I—"

"We can't do anything. The time will come and I'll have to ride out. I may only send you a note. I can't have anyone hurt over my personal problems."

"These people would defend you."

"And someone would get hurt. No, I'll just drift on when they come for me."

"How can they know you're here?"

"I don't know. One of those cowboys we stripped and sent out of here with only a raincoat to wear will talk about me in some saloon or cat house. They've got their ways, and nothing else to do but track me down."

She buried her face in his chest and hugged him. "I will burn candles at the sanctuary for you."

"Don't lose any sleep, but thanks."

"Will you ever ride by here again?" She threw her head back, and he could see the diamond-shaped tears on her cheeks.

"No."

She nodded that she'd heard his answer and swallowed hard. "Goddammit!" Then she halfheartedly hit him on the shoulder with her fist. "You're so damn stubborn."

"We better get dressed. I can hear the fandango has started down there."

"Yes, they will expect us." She lighted a candle lamp for them to see by.

"Rafael should be in San Antonio by now," he said,

pulling on his britches. He hooked the galluses over his shoulder and watched her put her arms in her dress and then shake it down over her figure. Damn shame he'd ever have to leave such a torrid woman. Maybe he would cut up through the Nation. He knew a dark-eyed Creek widow up on the Arkansas. Where he could rest his horse, reset the shoes on his pony and cut her some firewood—'less she'd found herself a man since the last time.

Index fingers hooked in the mule ears, he stuffed his toes in his boot with some effort and at last stomped his foot in it. She came across the room brushing her dark hair as he pulled on the second one.

"Will you leave when the Ranger arrives?"

He shook his head. "You ever seen an Appaloosa horse?"

"No."

"Well, this Kansas deputy's horse I'm talking about is mostly black and he has a white blanket with black spots over his rump. Big, good-looking, powerful animal that carries his head a little high—you can't miss him. Belongs to the Kansas deputy Ferd Abbott."

She shook her head and closed her eyes. With her hands, she swept her hair together and had him tie it in a ribbon.

"Will I look all right?"

"You look beautiful. Why?"

"Sometimes you wonder living on the inside of this body."

"I didn't tell you that to ruin your evening. I wanted you to know."

"Thank you," she said, taking his arm and looking back over the room. "Come, my ghost man. I want as much of you as I can get before you leave. I hope you're rested."

He grinned at her. "Ready for the war."

"You'll think war." Then she elbowed him in the ribs.

•   •   •

Montez came by and with a head toss drew him back in the shadows of the yard.

"This is Señor Penta." He motioned at a shorter man dressed in a suit. "He saw Rafael on the road. He was riding hard for San Antonio."

"Good."

The man nodded then spoke softly. "But behind him a couple of hours were two of McKlein's deputies on sweaty horses. I think they were after him."

"Shit." Slocum looked at the dark sky for help.

"What should we do?" Montez asked.

"I better ride for San Antonio. Saddle the big gray horse; he's the fastest and hottest blooded one." He turned to the man and shook his hand. "I appreciate the information, amigo. Thanks."

"Be careful. All these people around here are counting on you."

"I will be." He wet his cracked lips. Damn, he'd have to tell her. He dreaded that more than anything else. Already upset over the mention of his having to ride out one day, she'd not take this trip that he must make as a good thing either.

He swept her up by the arm and steered her back in the shadows beside the main house. Montez had already sent a boy to saddle the gray for him.

"What's wrong?" She frowned at him.

"I just got word that Rafael may not have made it to San Antonio."

"Huh?"

"Señor Penta is here. He saw two of McKlein's deputies riding hard on Rafael's backtrail."

"What are you—oh, no. Slocum, send someone else—please?"

"No, I'll get through. You keep the main crew here at the ranch and the gates guarded. Bixby may get some help hired and be desperate enough to charge in here anyday."

"Oh, please?"

"Is that rifle on him loaded?" he asked Montez, indicating one in the scabbard of the high-strung gray dancing around at the edge of the crowd.

The foreman went to check it. He nodded as they made small talk.

"Will I ever see you again?" she asked in the voice of a schoolgirl.

"I can't promise you anything. But I swear I'll do my damndest to get back here and see you again."

She hugged him, the wetness of her tears soaking into his shirt. Others gathered around and he nodded to them. "We have word that Rafael may have been ambushed or arrested."

The men and women bobbing their heads at him wore solemn looks. The music stopped. Only the creaking sizzle of the locusts cut the night.

"I'm going to get your vest," Amanda said and started for the house. "Don't leave until I get it?"

"I won't." He turned to the crowd. "There is a time to dance and sing, the psalms say. Start the music and dance, my friends. Tonight we dance and sing. I'll be back in three days with a Texas Ranger. He will stop this crazy man and you can go back to your work. Now dance! Sing!"

He led the gray toward the house, and the fandango started again, but he could hear none of the excitement of before. It pained him, but there was nothing he could do. If he hadn't been there when Bixby brought the cannon, the cannoneers might have leveled the ranch headquarters. He hoped they could defend the place till he returned. Damn.

17

Bixby began to pace the porch. His man Kerby Jones was sitting his horse waiting for his orders.

"Jones, I want every man armed and ready to ride in the morning. We're taking that damn Debaca place tomorrow."

Bixby coughed up a big hocker from his throat and spat in the dirt. "How many men can we have?"

"Call in the windmill guards, too?"

In rage, he scowled at his man. "I want everyone can sit a damn horse."

"Thirty."

"Have them ready to ride at daylight. We'll kill every one of them if they resist us."

"Yes, sir, Colonel."

With a nod of approval, Bixby headed for the front door. Lots to think about and plan. He went to study the map of that area on the wall in his office. He was back in his commander days again as the shaft of sunlight came through a field of dancing dust. McKlein should be there to help him. This hacienda he had promised to the sheriff. Why that lawman was so fascinated with owning that two-story house he would never know. But he had been, ever since they first talked about dividing the spoils of this country. Maybe McKlein had changed his mind about the place, but Bixby doubted it.

A glass of whiskey in his hand, he backed away from the map. As he leaned back in his chair, the springs creaked. For him the greatest prize would be Bonito Creek—then he would hold the entire country—and ah, Señora Debaca for his own plaything. Speaking of playthings, where was his Edora?

"Edora!" he shouted.

No answer.

He called her name again.

No answer. He shrugged his shoulders and got up to pour himself another whiskey. The new drink in his hand, he went back to the kitchen.

"Lupe, where is that girl?"

"I haven't seen her all morning long, señor."

"You see her, tell her to get her ass in there."

"Sí, señor."

That little bitch was hiding. He'd find her and beat her bare ass with a quirt. She needed a good lesson anyway. He looked out the window and wondered where she could be. Never mind, he had business to do. She'd show up in a few hours—if she'd been out screwing one of his gunhands, he would beat her butt till it was raw. Damn her, where was she?

No one had seen Edora all day when he took his supper. At least that's what they told him. The notion of her disappearance niggled him. But he was busy meeting with Jones and getting his plans all set for the action against Debaca's place. Past ten o'clock, he dropped in bed, even more angry that Edora wasn't there to service his throbbing erection. Where had she run off to?

Dawn, he awoke and strained to empty his bladder through his turgid shaft. No time to find anyone. The kitchen help were so old or ugly—damn, he would beat that little whore until she'd know better than to ever leave him again.

He dressed in a good business suit for his position as their leader. A toothless old hag brought his breakfast on a tray and interrupted his thinking about the glory of his victory over the ranch defenders. The food turned to paste in his mouth. Sunbeams coming through the front door crept across the worn floorboards. He choked down some too hot coffee and shoved the food aside. This plan to take the place had to work.

When his army left the ranch, he rode at the front of the column. Jones had sent two men ahead to scout the place. Good man, that Jones. He had more men like him, this job would be over. A fresh breath of the cedar's pungent aroma swept Bixby's face. He could taste his victory. Men, guns and plenty of ammo—it would be a sweet day.

"Someone's coming," Jones said, riding in at his side.

His hand on his pistol butt, Bixby nodded.

"My scouts," Jones said and booted his horse forward to meet the pair.

"What is it?" Jones shouted.

"The damn place is deserted."

"Deserted?" Bixby drove his horse into their midst.

"I'm telling you there ain't a damn soul there. Kinda spooky."

"Where in the hell did they go?" Bixby demanded.

"Be goddamned if I know," the scout called Tony said. "They wiped out their tracks or drove some animals over them."

Slocum—what in the hell are you up to now? Bixby narrowed his eyes, gritted his teeth and clenched his fist. *I'll get you, you dirty, no-good bastard.*

18

Slocum short loped the gray through the silvery open parts of the road and swung wide of any community that might report his travels to Bixby or the sheriff that he didn't trust either. Making good time, he crossed the shallow river where he'd first met Bixby and they'd fought. He let the gray drink and blow.

In five minutes, he was back alternating trotting and short loping the big horse. The sharp aroma of campfire smoke forced him to rein down the gelding and search the inky night for the source. His ear turned to listen, and he patted the gray on his wet neck as he snorted and tossed his head with impatience. No need to signal his arrival, if it was the two deputies.

Another snoot full of the smoke and he hitched the gray to a cedar bow. He jerked the Winchester out of the scabbard and headed around the pungent-smelling evergreen. A few yards later he could see the blazing campfire. He counted two men and the prisoner, then a third joined them. The bare-headed one seated in the firelight and bound by handcuffs was Rafael.

Damn those three. What excuse had they used to arrest

him? Didn't need one—he had to be an inconvenience to them. Slocum drew the hammer back on the Winchester until it clicked. For two bits he'd turn the pair into buzzard bait. Lawmen—they didn't even resemble lawmen, let alone act like them.

Slocum moved in closer, making his way slow and careful toward them. He could hear them talking at last.

"You better get ready, boy," the thicker-set deputy said to Rafael. "They hang horse thieves in Texas. Especially Mexican ones." Then he laughed loud—a big, haughty sound that carried in the night. "Yeah, stretch your skinny neck until your face turns purple and you poop in your pants."

Rafael didn't answer his tormentor. Only sat there in the firelight, acting unperturbed by the situation except for an occasional glance down at the bracelets on his wrists.

"Grab some stars!" Slocum told them.

The three deputies jumped up in the firelight, but they had the caution to raise their hands quickly.

"You must be Slocum," the bearded one said. "You ain't getting through. We've got guards set up all along the way to San Antonio."

"Where're the keys to those cuffs?" Slocum demanded, not doubting that shutting off any leakage of information to the authorities was the primary goal of the sheriff and the Colonel.

"We ain't got them."

"Then use your teeth and go to biting the chain between his hands in two."

"Ha!"

"Find those keys and fast or you won't have any teeth behind those whiskers."

"Here," the bearded one said and reached in his vest pocket. He tossed the keys on the ground and Rafael swept them up.

"I'm glad to see you, señor."

"Slocum," he corrected the man. "Get their guns, then handcuff them together. Each facing a different way."

"Why's that?" the bearded one frowned at him.

"So one of you can walk forward and one can walk backward."

"You can't—"

"Shut up," Rafael said, squeezing the cuff tight on the man's wrist. "It will be a good way for you and your no-good partners to walk." With that said, he swift-like kneed the big man hard in the crotch. "How does that feel to you, son of a bitch?"

Rafael caught the other wide-eyed deputy, whirled him around and cuffed his wrist so he faced away from his partner. "You're lucky, *bastardo*. I should have cut both of your nuts off."

"I never—"

The bearded one straightened up, and before Slocum could warn his man, he made a grab for Rafael. Not quick enough, though—the vaquero gave him a boot toe in the balls that made him scream, then drop to his knees doubling over his privates and hollering in pain.

"They got horses?" Slocum asked.

"*Sí*, I will get them." Rafael took off on the run and returned leading four horses.

"We've got a long ways to go. They say there are more guards. We'll have to be careful."

"*Sí, señor.* I thought I was by them. So I got on the road."

"Can we find a back way?" Slocum tossed his head at the deputies, not wanting them to hear.

"It will take a long time," Rafael whispered.

"I'd rather get there alive. They'll have lots of people out looking for us. We probably have sizeable rewards on our heads."

Rafael nodded. "Let's ride."

• • •

At daylight, they came down a long canyon, the dim wagon tracks lined with thick live oaks. Slocum could hear goats and chickens ahead.

"Whose place is this?"

"A cousin of Tina's. Her name is Erlene." Rafael smiled like he knew something. "She will like you."

"We safe here?" Slocum didn't give a damn what she liked—he was tired from all night skirting through the hills to avoid detection.

"Oh, very safe. She won't tell anyone. We can stay here till sundown," Rafael said.

A couple of dogs went to barking and a dark-haired woman appeared in the doorway of the jacal, wearing a *pistola* on her hip. She was smoking a corn-husk cigarette. Her full breasts pushed hard on the thin dress material and the deep cleavage looked like a canyon.

"What do you bastards want?" she asked, looking narrow-eyed at them and twisting her shoulders in a sullen way.

"We want to buy some food and take a few hours' rest," Rafael said.

"I know him." She tossed her head at Rafael. "Who in the fuck are you?"

"He's Señor—"

"Shut up, donkey dick, he can talk for himself."

"Howdy." Slocum dropped from the saddle, pulled the crotch of his pants down and undid the girth on the gelding. "My name's Slocum." Then he undid the bull-hide chaps, hung them on the saddle horn, took off his spurs and did the same with them.

"Slocum," she said and looked at him haughtily.

Rafael started for the door of her jacal and went by her to search inside. Then when she turned, looking indignant at him, he reached back and gave her a hard swat on the ass with his hand. She bolted forward with a sharp scream. Ignoring her swearing, he gave a head toss for Slocum to come on.

Rafael scowled at the woman. "Fix us some food. Where's a place to wash up?"

"Over there. I could blow your ass off, you know that?"

"You were going to do that you'd've already done it, Erlene." He poured water into a pan.

"What are you doing here, donkey dick?"

He stopped washing his hands and looked pained at her. "Quit yakking and fix some food. We're starved."

Slocum suppressed a grin and edged around her to join him at the washbasin.

"Men! They always are the ruination of my life." She shook her fist at the stick-and-wattle roof. "Slo-cum, why do you come here?"

"So he can hide out from that crooked sheriff and Bixby and get to San Antonio to contact the Rangers to come get them."

"What is so hard about that? I mean, how many men do they have?"

"Many," Rafael said. "They shot Pedro, the boy. Slocum had to get him back from them. Then they jumped me and if he hadn't come along—"

She smiled, came over with a parry knife in her hand, put the toe of her foot on the edge of a chair, drew her dress up so it exposed her shapely brown leg and for effect pointed the knife at them. "Those hombres need to be skinned and nailed on a fence."

"I told you she would be glad to see us," Rafael said, like she wasn't even there.

She turned and frowned at Rafael. Must be a story there, Slocum decided.

"I would like that boy of Bixby's skinned, too," she said.

"He's dead." Rafael made a face behind his mustache.

"Who did it?" She looked back and forth at them.

"Slocum did it."

"For that I owe you a toss in the bed, hombre." Her dark slits for eyes met his and she nodded.

"Fix us some food. We're hungry now," Rafael said, drying his hands.

"Hmm," she snorted out her rather slender nose, which had a small bridge like she must have once broken it. "You men are all hungry or horny."

"Right now we're hungry."

She soon stirred a skillet sizzling with onions, squash and peppers. While the griddle steamed, she made flour tortillas with her hands, using her palm to occasionally test the heat of the black metal sheet she planned to cook them on. On her knees she worked swiftly. The aroma of her cooking soon filled the casa as they sat on crates. From a pot she drew out strips of marinated meat and added them to her skillet.

"The last of the goat I butchered," she said.

Both men nodded that they heard her, and observed the cooking operation.

"How is my cousin Tina who lives at the ranch?" she asked.

"Fine. I think she is pregnant again," Rafael said.

Erlene wrinkled her nose and stirred the frying food. "She likes babies."

In minutes, she served them some thick recooked frijoles, her skillet full of steaming hot vegetables and meat, with piles of tortillas to wrap it all in. They ate in silence, but Slocum knew he was being inspected as she looked hard at him over the tortilla each time she took a bite.

"Where are you from?" Erlene asked between mouthfuls.

"Other places."

"I know that."

"I came down from Oregon."

"Ah, what is it like up there?" she asked, taking another bite of her food.

"Lots of forest. Pines in the mountains."

"You see the ocean?"

He shook his head. "Never was that far west."

She looked disappointed. "I want to see that once."

"What the hell for?" Rafael asked.

" 'Cause I ain't never seen it, stupid."

Rafael shook his head in disgust. "You have a perfectly good farm here your husband left you."

"Oh, yes, donkey dick. A wonderful place. You see any chandeliers hanging over your head? That polished staircase? I have a two-bit goat ranch and I don't have any *dinero* to buy silk dresses to wear when I go to the Gulf and see the fine sand."

"Screwing in that sand would make you sore," he said and laughed.

She made a bad face at him and spoke to Slocum. "He is an idiot."

Slocum smiled and shook his head at their conversation. Her fresh food drew the saliva to his mouth and her obviously inviting actions seated cross-legged in front of him made him think about her ample body.

At once she looked around the hard-packed floor as if she'd forgot something, and rose to her feet in an exposure of her bare legs. "I'll get us some wine."

"Good. I was about to choke," Rafael said and took another big bite.

The red wine served in tin cups, she took her place again. "How far away is Oregon?" she asked Slocum.

"Two thousand miles or more."

"Your ass get sore riding a horse that far?"

"Sometimes."

She looked at the ceiling. "Mine aches thinking about it."

"Where do we sleep?" Rafael asked.

"You can sleep on that pallet." She pointed to one in the corner. "He can sleep in the hammock out back."

"You must be the honored guest," Rafael said, undoing his gunbelt.

Slocum nodded and considered the wine left in his cup. They better get some rest and try to push on into San Antonio during the night. "We'll leave here at sundown."

"*Sí,*" Rafael agreed and headed for the pallet.

Slocum downed the rest of his wine and she took him by the hand. "I'll show you the hammock."

"Good," he said and rose. She led him outside into the glaring sun, then up a small pathway to a hilltop and into a shady grove. The day's heat was beginning to rise—a soft wind swept the glen, and while the temperature would increase as the day went on, he knew this was the best place to sleep.

He nodded in approval at the wide swing. It would be much cooler out there than in the jacal.

"Get your clothes off," she said in a low voice and began undoing the buttons down the front of her blouse, spilling her melon-size breasts out of the garment.

She wore nothing under it, he decided, toeing off his boots and watching her shed the skirt. Below the slight rise of her belly was the darkest, thickest bush of pubic hair he'd ever seen. When she dropped her butt on the hammock, her actions caused her great boobs to quake.

When he'd finished hanging his clothes and holster on the stubby limbs, he heard her suck in her breath.

"This may be better than the ocean," she said and rolled over into the swinging bed.

Her legs spread apart, she pulled him on top of her. "Put it in. Oh, my, I can hardly wait. My. My. . . ."

The feel of her calloused fingers directing his half-hard dick into her added to the stimulus. Though wet with her fluids, the entry was tight and grew even tighter as he pumped it into her. His erection quickly became stone hard and stiff.

A great sigh escaped her lips and she bit his chest near the left shoulder. As she hunched her ass forward for all of him, his pubic bone soon nestled against the dense brush and they were lost in the fiery passion.

His legs ached with cramps and she groaned and grunted as she fought for more and more. The world around them spun like a top, and he pounded her until at last he felt the gnawing pain in his gonads and the rise of the hot flow toward her. His world dimmed and she cried, "Yes!"

She arched her back for him, raising off his knees on the springy hammock. The head of his skintight wand exploded and they fell into a sweaty pile. At last the rising wind swept over their bare skin, cooling them. Slocum fell asleep.

A dog barking woke him. Half-asleep, he rolled out of the swinging hammock, bare feet on the dirt, and hurried over for his pistol. He could see nothing out of place, but something warned him. It wasn't right. He slipped on his pants and then he heard the shots from below.

What the hell was going on? Must be close to noontime, he decided. He sat on the ground to jerk on his boots. With all the stickers and goat heads, he had no intention of trying to move about barefooted. The shots had come from the jacal, but he couldn't see a thing from his place in the trees. He put on the shirt and vest, never buttoned it, and with his hat on his head and his six-gun in hand, he headed down the path for her casa.

Then he spotted several men on horses. He ducked behind a cedar with wide boughs and could hear someone ranting. "That sumbitch Slocum ain't here. He must be on his way to San Anton."

"Let's ride. That bastard gets there, we're all done for."

"Them two ain't talking."

Slocum winced. They must have shot Rafael and Erlene. What could he do? There were half a dozen riders down there milling around making lots of dust. Somehow he needed to get to San Antonio—if he couldn't do anything for the two of them.

"Let's ride. We've got to check some more places!" the leader shouted and they galloped away.

At last, when he looked inside the jacal, Slocum shook his head at the sight of her naked body sprawled on her back on the floor. Blood covered her face and he bent over to close her wide open eyes. A naked Rafael stretched out on his side near by her, several wounds seeping blood from his back and chest when Slocum rolled him over. Inches from his open fingers lay his Colt. He was dead, too.

Shaken by the wanton butchery, Slocum buttoned his shirt and went back to the doorway for a breath of fresh air. That rotten bunch would pay for this. He needed to wrap their bodies, then find someone to bury them. Without a guide, he'd have a hard time reaching San Antonio in any short while. Rafael had known this back way. For him to take the main road would be far too dangerous; if they'd found her isolated place, there was no telling how many hired guns they had out looking for him.

He secured the bodies in blankets and barred the door so animals couldn't get inside. Then he saddled the gray and wondered why they'd never noticed his horse and saddle. They were in a rush, he guessed. The gray and Rafael's horse were both in a trap and somewhat out of sight. Perhaps they'd dismissed the second horse as hers was all he could think—damn, it was a waste to shoot those two.

On the road east, he met some firewood gatherers with an empty train of donkeys, a grandfather, father and two sons. He paid them twenty pesos for the burial detail and they promised to do it properly. The money represented a large sum of cash for them and they started out at once, saying they knew the señora and her place well.

Leaving them, he stood in the stirrups and trotted the

gray. Close to sundown, he stopped to water the gelding in a shallow crossing.

"Don't make a move. We've got you covered."

Slocum closed his eyes and sunk in the seat of the saddle. *Damn!*

19

"Sheriff sent me," the out-of-breath deputy said. "To tell you he's got Slocum. Brought him in last night."

"Dead, I hope?" Bixby asked, standing in his robe on the porch in the morning sun.

The deputy leaned over to talk softer. "Got him drugged. McKlein intends to try him and send him up. Then no one can say he didn't follow the law, if they do send Rangers up here."

"Risky damn business. You tell him he can move into the Debaca place anytime. We cleared it out yesterday."

The deputy smiled and agreed to inform the sherrif.

Bixby watched him ride out. He rubbed an itch in his upper lip. This new woman Nora was a poor replacement in bed for that traitorous bitch Edora. He'd learned when he returned, after some serious threats and torture of the house women, that when Edora overheard his plans to take the hacienda, she'd quickly slipped away, ridden over there and warned them.

"What did that one know?" Jones asked, coming from the bunkhouse area as McKlein's man rode out.

"They have Slocum as a prisoner in jail." Bixby

coughed up some phlegm and spat it out, watching the deputy ride off.

"They going to kill him when he tries to escape?"

"Maybe. They've got him drugged and are going to try him."

"What the hell for?"

"To cover McKlein's ass, I think, so if the Rangers come and investigate."

"Crazy to me. I've got all the crews out rebranding all of her cattle."

"Good. The sooner we get that done the better. Any idea where those hacienda people went?"

"Snake says they went into the hills and are hiding in caves."

"We need to get about six good men and start eliminating them."

"I know, but I've got all the hands out rebranding—"

Bixby nodded. "I know you do, but we must do that next. Are all the windmills running?"

"Most all. I think they're still disconnecting some. But I have several men working to keep them pumping."

He used his index finger to point at Jones. "You catch any sumbitch wrecking a windmill, or even think he has, you hang him. I want to make living examples out of those bastards."

"I'll do it."

"Good." Maybe he should ride into town and converse with McKlein a little about what he intended to do with his prisoner. No, let that bastard come out there and talk to him. He had delivered McKlein his part of the deal. The Debaca place was his. If only they had taken her hostage— he would be screwing her fine ass instead of this loose pussy he shared his bed with—blah.

Amanda Debaca, I am saving the best for you.

20

"He pleads guilty," Sheriff McKlein said.

"Can the defendant stand up?" the judge behind the desk asked.

"We can hold him up," McKlein said and motioned to the two guards to do so.

Slocum felt them lift him by the arms out of the chair. Far off in the distance he heard the judge's voice. "John Doe, I find you guilty of two counts of murder in the first degree. You are hereby sentenced to hang in two weeks."

"Why so fucking long?" McKlein shouted.

"'Cause it has to be filed in Austin."

"Hell, morning wouldn't be soon enough."

"Dammit, McKlein, it ain't your neck on the line. It could be mine."

"Ain't no one going to miss this pistolero."

Slocum felt his head swing sideways. He was so doped that he couldn't speak anything understandable through his lips. Sentenced to hang. What a mess. He had to get better. But how?

They led him back to the jail cell, off by itself. No window, no light, and it smelled like piss, but he smelled like that, too, since he couldn't get up and relieve himself. He lay on the iron pallet and listened. About the time he would revive, the next food serving or even the water they gave him would be loaded with some kind of dope. Probably laudanum.

A twenty-four-hour guard sat in a captain's chair in the outer room with a shotgun across his lap. There was another solid steel door beyond him, then the sheriff's office that bristled with armed deputies. That much he'd noted being taken from the jail to the judge's office and back.

He worried about Amanda's situation and what was happening at the ranch. If only he had the strength to do something.

"I'm getting a couple of Mexican women to come in here to wash his ass up," McKlein said to his guard in the hall. "He's stinking up the whole goddamn office out here, and they can wash down the cell, too. Make sure he don't try anything. Son of a bitch, I ought to hang him right now."

"Be good enough for him."

"He still out from the last dose?" McKlein asked.

"Yeah."

"Thought it would kill him—"

"Naw. He's tough as rawhide."

"You're right, Earl. Just watch them bitches good that are coming to clean him and this piss pot up."

"He ain't getting out of here."

"Just be goddamn sure he don't, or I'll hang your ass." McKlein laughed aloud.

Slocum drifted off into la-la land again.

He felt them washing him and whispering to each other when he began to awaken. They rolled him over and the water felt cold as they scrubbed his privates and then dried them.

"He's about dead," one whispered.

"His dick is, too," the other hissed and about laughed.

"Just clean him up. You want to suck on something, come suck on mine," the deputy said.

"Oh, really?"

"Yeah, really."

"Oh, could I?"

"Damn right. Get over here, honey."

Slocum's vision was foggy, but he could see the big-gutted guard set the shotgun across the chair, stand up and undo his pants, spilling his privates out. The woman bent down and Slocum suspected she took his dick in her hand.

Then the guard sucked in his breath. "Oh Jesus, be easy with that knife."

"Slocum, Slocum, wake up," someone said in his ear. But he couldn't answer.

Their rescue of him from the jail was all fading in and out. He was taken by strong arms, and he saw several of the guards bound and gagged in chairs as they sprinted him through the outer office. Then he was put on a pallet in a wagon bed, and the thing rumbled away. All the time he could hear in the distance some woman's voice saying, "You've got to live."

21

Bixby sat half-asleep in his desk chair. Slocum had escaped from the jail. That bitch Edora had warned them at the ranch. He had his men on the lookout for her. When he got through with her—a smile came to the corner of his mouth—he would have every man on the ranch screw her in one night. She'd learn what giving aid to the enemy earned her. Ha ha.

Some riders had ridden up from the direction of town. He could make them out though the lace curtains. Maybe McKlein was with them. About time that he came by and thanked Bixby for the Debaca place. Bixby rose and stretched. What the hell—in a week or so, when this all settled down, he'd go to San Anton and find him a new plaything. That dreadful whore he slept with was driving him crazy—she talked all the time. All the time.

He stood in the open front doorway and studied the three men. One was a prisoner.

"Who the hell is he?" he asked the deputy about the man bound up on the center horse.

"A Ranger. McKlein wants him kept on ice until he figures what to do with him."

"Shoot him and bury his carcass."

"No, McKlein wants him held until he says what to do with him."

"You boys let Slocum get away. Guess it would be a good idea to have him out here."

"Them bitches—"

"Did those bitches really castrate that guard?"

The stern-faced deputy, doing all the talking, nodded. "It wasn't funny either."

Bixby shrugged. "If he'd been doing his job, it would never have happened."

"All the same we know who that bitch is. We'll get her one of these days."

"Jones," Bixby shouted, seeing his man by the horses. "You've got a prisoner to guard. McKlein can't keep them in his jail."

"Yes sir, Boss. We can handle him."

"What's his name?" Bixby asked.

"Troy Graham."

"Well, Graham, welcome to the Bixby Ranch."

The prisoner glared back at him, Jones leading him by the shoulder. "Bixby, you and the rest of these bastards better go to saying your prayers. Texas Rangers get through with you, you'll all need new assholes or coffins."

"Mighty tough talk for a man awaiting his own execution. You better start praying." Bixby waved Jones on. He had no desire to hear all that crap. "Tell McKlein we need to talk," he said to the sheriff's deputy.

The man nodded that he'd heard him and they turned their horses back toward town. Good riddance, Bixby decided. Those stupid deputies had no idea he was the one who paid their salaries. Maybe he'd take a nap.

The Ranger was locked up in the shed, guards posted. Slocum might be out of jail, but he would find this place bristled this time with security. There would be no raids on Bixby's ranch that were not fended off. *Bring your damn dumb Messikins to die.*

He met with Jones the next morning over breakfast. "How's the prisoner?"

"Tough acting as ever. What do you want out of him?"

"We'll let McKlein decide that. We're only holding him for the sheriff."

"My two scouts, Vester and McKillvin, think they may have found the cave that she's hid in."

"Wonderful. Let's saddle up and go get her."

Jones shook his head. "They think they can nab her without a fight and then those stupid greasers of hers will give up."

"You forget about Slocum?" Bixby considered his china cup of coffee.

"He tries to come after her, he's a dead duck. I ain't pulling no fancy things like McKlein tried and get screwed up."

"If they get Debaca here to me unharmed, I'll pay both of them two hundred in gold. You, too." Bixby didn't want that filthy breed Vester sticking his dick in her, or the red-headed scotsman likewise.

"I mean I'll only pay it if she's unharmed."

Jones smiled at the mention of the money. His mouth did anyway; his eyes held the harsh coldness of a wolf. Never mind his disposition, Jones was the best commander in the field Bixby had had since the war.

When Jones left, Bixby drank some fine whiskey. To celebrate, for soon he was going to have that dark-eyed bitch in his clutches at last. Looking out the window at the yard, he saw Jones talking to the two scouts. Amanda Debaca, your ass will be in my bed soon. Ha ha.

The two delivered her to him the next afternoon. Vester wore a bandanna bandage around his head. The redheaded Scotsman was hatless, too, and looked the worse from wear. She sat straight-backed in the saddle with her mussed hair full of grass and sticks. She tossed it aside to glare at him. Prayer-like, her hands were bound tight before her by rope.

"You got our money?" Vester asked, jerking her off the horse and dragging her toward the house.

"How about double or nothing?" Bixby asked, looking with excitement at the filthy woman standing not twenty feet from him with the sullen glare in her eyes.

"How's that?" McKillvin asked with a frown.

"I'll pay you each five hundred dollars for Slocum's scalp and her."

"What if we don't get him?"

"Then I don't owe you for her."

"I'll take my money now." The redhead stuck out his hand. Vester agreed and did the same.

He paid them. "Get Slocum now."

They nodded. Bixby stepped forward for his purchase, took her by the arm and dragged her toward the house. Despite her efforts to resist, he brought her inside and closed the door with a slam that rattled the glass.

"At last, you fucking bitch, you are going to be mine."

She bared her teeth and tried to kick him with her bare foot. He slapped her backhanded and forward, dazing her.

"I like breaking in mean bitches. I'll really like breaking you."

"Go to hell—" His cuff to her face silenced her words. Then he jerked her up close and forced his mouth to hers. She tasted of horse and sweat, but that only fueled the fire inside him. He wanted her and he would have her.

He dragged her into the bedroom and closed the door, locking it with the key. After a bath, she would be elegant, but he liked the notion of this wildcat. Dirt, horse smell and rebellion—he could hardly wait. Better leave her hands tied the first time.

Better yet, tie them over her head to the bed's headboard. First he would rip the clothes off her body—that would make her embarrassed, and he knew she'd then be easier to handle. The realization that they had no clothes on, and that anyone could see all of them, made them suddenly less able to fend him off. He had done it many times to virgins and inexperienced women.

He began to shred her clothing. He tore the blouse open and fondled her pendulous breasts. She tried to fight him, but he soon held her hands with one and felt them with the other for his own pleasure.

"Ah, such fine tits you have."

"You bastard—you will pay for this . . ."

He had to use his pocketknife to shred the clothes, so soon she was naked and downcast-looking on the bed. He unbuckled his belt and stripped it out, then grasped her wrists, forcing her onto her back, and bound her hands over her head to the headboard.

She tried to kick him with her dirty feet, but it did no good—he only laughed at her. Undressing, he looked at her curled in a fetal ball with her arms outstretched. For so long he had imagined this moment. Undressed at last, he spread her strong legs apart so he was soon between them.

Seething with rage, she twisted and cursed him, but he held her legs apart and drove his great dick inside her. Then he began to smile with the success of his efforts to pump deeper and deeper into her. *Now struggle, you bitch.* He knew that before long her own body would deceive her, and she would be in his power then.

"No—no," she cried and he knew his efforts had begun to move her. He grasped the cheeks of her ass and drove himself farther and farther into her, feeling the hardness of her swollen clit on his rod. Her back began to arch toward him and her eyes began to look glazed. Then he felt the contractions in her vagina. Ah, now, bitch, you are mine.

He came, and she collapsed in a pile. He rose up and turned her over. He reached between her legs, underneath her, and filled his hand with the slick fluids seeping from her. He spread her legs apart as she lay facedown and applied the goo to her crack. Then before she could coil up, he stuck his hard-on in her ass.

His hand muffled her screams as he forcefully drove the head painfully home. The small aperture finally gave to his stone erection and the force of his muscular butt driving the spike home. At last, he was inside her, pumping harder and harder. She fainted. His teeth clenched, and he strained hard until at last he came again, then collapsed on top of her. Oh, he was going to have fun with her body.

He went to the washbasin and cleaned up. He better put her in the shed with the Ranger for the rest of the day. He lathered the blood and mess on his privates, looking at the black hair on his broad chest in the mirror on the dresser. He rinsed out the rag, took off the soap and remains and then dried himself. There was a robe in the closet that would fit her. He'd untie her hands, put the robe on her and then retie them. She couldn't be trusted for a while—but eventually he'd break her will.

After dressing her and retying her hands, he dragged her to the front door and shouted for a guard to come get her.

"Yes sir, Mr. Bixby."

A new boy they'd just hired. He didn't even know Bixby was "Colonel" to his hired help.

"Put her in the shed, with that Ranger. Anyone screws her, I'll cut their dick off with an ax. Savvy?"

"Yes, sir."

"Tell all the other guards that, too."

"I will, sir."

He watched the boy jerk her along. About dark he'd be ready for another dose of her. Much better than that last bitch. Ha ha.

22

Slocum opened his dry eyes. It was dark wherever he was at. Then he made out a nearby fire and saw how it lighted the cavern roof over him. Where in the hell was he at? Why couldn't he shake the grogginess in his brain?

"Ah, you finally awake?" a woman asked.

"Yeah," he managed in a voice that shocked him.

"I am Tia. They have been drugging you."

"I know. They had a trial and I never even spoke a word."

"Kangaroo court. Bixby has taken the ranch."

"Where are all the ranch people?" he asked.

"A girl named Edora from Bixby's ranch warned us he was bringing many men to take the ranch the next day. Montez decided we should let them have it, so that they did not kill the women and children."

"Good idea. Where are the others at?"

"They are hiding in caves. The men are trying to stop them from rebranding all her cattle."

"The Rangers?" he managed to ask.

"The Rangers are up their ass, I guess. We finally got word to them and still no one has come."

"Where's Amanda?"

"That is the bad news. Two of his men kidnapped her yesterday from another cave while we were getting you up here." She chewed on her lower lip.

"Do you know where she is?"

"We think they have her at Bixby's ranch."

"How many men can ride?"

"Perhaps a dozen, counting boys. Many of them are out there trying to stop the rebranding of her cattle."

"I know . . . I know you all must have had hell." Exhausted from his exertion to sit up on the pallet, he tried to open his mind to thinking what to do next about Amanda.

"Here is some coffee, maybe that will help you."

He agreed with a nod and accepted the cup. Whatever they used on him had been powerful and he needed to sober up. He blew on the steam to cool it.

"Where is Montez?"

"The ones who kidnapped her—they killed him." The woman began to sob.

Slocum wanted to comfort her, but he could hardly sit up, let alone get up and hug the woman. He sprawled back on his hands and stiff arms to brace himself. "They will pay for this. What's your name?"

"Tia," she managed between her tears.

"Yes, I should have remembered that. Tia, call a meeting. Is it night now?"

"Yes."

"Call a meeting for tomorrow here for all the men that can fight. Maybe by then I can think clear enough."

"I will call on some women, too."

"The ones who helped me escape?" He realized then that the women had handled his getaway. In his groggy condition, he could not recall a man being with them.

"Good," she said, wiping at her tears. "Everyone said you would know what to do when you were off those drugs."

"Who?"

"The women of the ranch."

"Did you cut that jail deputy's balls off?" he asked her with a smile.

"If you see him again he may talk in a high-pitched voice," she said. "That bastard."

"I'm going to have to sleep awhile longer. Wake me up in time to meet with them." He set the half-drunk cup aside and lowered himself down on the pallet. No strength, he needed to get his back.

She covered him with a quilt.

When he awoke, he discovered that the cave held many who'd come to fight. He sat on the pallet with some of his thinking restored. He recognized many of the men's faces from the ranch. But the women impressed him as well; many wore bandoleers with ammunition and pistols. Several of the attractive ones had hacked their hair short.

The part-Apache who used the buffalo gun on the cannoneers squatted a few feet from him.

"Do they hold the señora at his ranch?" he asked the man.

The Apache nodded, his dark face a mask of anger.

"How many men guard her?" he asked.

"Many pistoleros."

Tia rose to her feet with a rifle in her hand and joined them. "We have some of our sisters who are working as spies at his ranch now. They are looking for a chance to get the señora free. They are very watchful. Oh, Bixby is also holding a young man—we think he's a Ranger."

"A Ranger?" Slocum asked. "Had they sent one?"

"Yes, but he is only a boy." The woman shook her head to dismiss his importance.

"There are lots of young men serving as Rangers. We need him out of there, too. He can get us some real help."

"What should we do to get this done?" A tall, slender woman standing at the side asked the question. She wore ammunition belts crisscrossed over her breasts. Her dark eyes bore holes in him.

"This woman talking to you, her name is Donna," Tia said in his ear.

"Donna, in the morning I will ride over and scout this place. And then we can decide."

"Señor." An older man stood up to speak. "His men are already rebranding her cattle like they own them."

"Are there guards with these crews?"

"Sí, señor."

"Are the men working those cattle vaqueros?"

"Sí."

"Can we trust any of these vaqueros?"

A tough-looking woman stood up wearing a six-gun in a holster on her hip. "Some we can, some we can't."

Others nodded.

"Then give the ones that will help us pistols to hide until we jump Bixby's guards."

That satisfied many, who nodded their heads in agreement with his plan.

"They guard even their horses now," a woman said. "Or we would have cut their girths like you did that night."

"Have you tried to distract them, these guards?" he asked with a knowing smile.

"No," the lady pointed at him, "but we will." Her words drew several laughs and smiles.

He bet they would.

"Let's find our friends in the workers and I will look over the Bixby setup."

"God be with you!" someone shouted, and a chorus added the same in the cavern's echoes.

So he needed to be strong enough by sunup to ride a horse and perhaps outrun some of Bixby's men. The people were leaving—many waved goodbye to him.

"I think he plans a cattle drive soon," the woman called Donna said, walking up.

"He probably needs the money to pay all these workers

and guards," Slocum said. "He must have an army-size payroll."

"He had not paid the ranch help in two months, until the other day."

"What about her money at the ranch?" He recalled that Amanda kept a large sum in an old green safe in her office.

"She took it and hid it. They never got it."

"Good. So it is safe?"

"Yes, and I have a good ranch horse for you to ride," Donna said. "I will go with you."

"Thanks," he said as Tia nodded her approval.

His head pounded with a headache. He wished it was clearer so he could think. Being doped up for the week had left him depleted and mindless—Amanda being held as a prisoner of Bixby made him angry and frustrated about his next move. They probably kept her under a strong guard, especially since the women broke him out of the county jail.

"You should rest," Tia said. "You will be stronger in the morning."

He shook his head to clear the cobwebs. She brought him some tea.

"Drink this. You will feel better."

The tin cup in his hands, he considered the fire's light casting shadows on the red rock walls of the cave. He glanced up at Tia. She stood above him with her arms folded and the serape over her shoulder against the cave's coolness.

A woman in her forties, the flickering reflection on her high cheekbones, the sadness in the corners of her eyes, she stared across the room. Moved by her taking charge of his fate, the jail breakout and all, he wondered what he should say to her.

"You approve of me going to look over Bixby's security?"

She glanced away then turned back. "I worry for the señora. She tried so hard . . ."

"I should never have left her."

"No. You were on a mission to save her and the ranch."

"I wish it had turned out different." He sipped the strong tea.

"Nothing you could have done. I tell you that this Donna is a *tigre*. She won't let anything happen to you unless they kill her."

"Good, thanks. I'll try to see that doesn't happen." He looked at the pallet underneath him. "I better get some sleep."

"Yes," she said. "You need your rest. I want to check and be sure the guard is on the lookout."

"Thanks," he said and lay down.

She whipped out another blanket and covered him. "I will wake you in time."

He acknowledged her words and closed his eyes. The next day would bring more problems. But even in his still-drugged dumb stupor he worried abut Amanda. *We are coming.*

23

"There goes that same *bastardo*," the willowy Donna said, lying belly down beside him, studying the ranch. "Twice he's taken food in that jacal."

Slocum's eye to the telescope, he agreed. "That must be where they are holding her."

"One fat one out in front sits in the chair with a rifle."

"You know him?" Slocum asked.

"They call him Kelly."

"You know that boy takes the food?"

In reply, she shook her head so hard she had to raise up to sweep the short hair from her face. She blew out a sharp breath through her pursed, full lips. "But if I could get up close, I could coax that Kelly away from his post."

"Too damn dangerous. After the jailbreak and castration, I bet they've been warned not to be tempted."

She squeezed her fist like she was crushing something in it. "That's what I would do to his balls."

"They want us to lose our cool. We need a better plan. How much hay do they have and where?"

"There is a stack by the corral. Why?"

"I'll explain. Can we get up on the house and stuff that chimney with wet sacks?"

Her dark eyes danced with mischief when she looked over at him. "You plan to really distract them?"

"We bring a big bunch here to fight them, they'll throw their forces at us and may kill her."

"What is first?"

"We cut the barb wire on the horse trap and let their ponies out the back way. You smell those pigs?"

She wrinkled her nose. "Yes."

"We let them out about dark. I can hear baby ones. Those sows will be pissed and mad. That will add to the confusion. We'll stop the kitchen chimney and set the hay on fire, then you can coax Kelly off his ass and I'll bust him over the head."

"What if they have guards inside the jacal, too?"

"Cross that bridge when we get there." He studied the house. Bixby had not shown himself. That was good, because without a commander they wouldn't organize as fast.

"I think I can slip up to those sheds and find the sacks," she said.

"How?" He frowned at the idea of her taking any unnecessary chances.

"I can come up that canyon over there and use the cedars for cover. The guard on the shed roof won't see me and I can have them ready for the job."

"Don't take any chances."

She made a kiss at him with her full lips then backed away under the juniper that sheltered them. "If I can't do it, I'll be back."

"Careful," he hissed after her.

He watched another gunslinger come by and jaw with Kelly. He wore a gunbelt and no doubt was part of the force, but not anyone important. He did toss his head toward the room and Kelly nodded. Though he couldn't hear them, the motion convinced Slocum that Amanda and that young Ranger were both in there.

He scoped out the guard with the rifle on top of the barn

roof, and wondered about him. Then he watched him come to the edge and talk to someone on the ground. A smile crossed Slocum's face because he saw Donna, with her dress above her knees, using the distraction to break for the barn, going beyond the two and out of their vision.

Good enough. She was in the barn, where she knew the whereabouts of the sacks. He studied the place, but the guard on the roof looked to be the only one visible and Slocum decided he must be the chief outlook, besides Kelly, who leaned back in his chair and kept an eye on things.

Then Slocum saw something different. It was Donna, taking clothes that were drying off the line. Then she faded out of view toward the barn and he resumed breathing again. What the hell was she doing?

He forced his eyes to stay open as the day warmed. He wished he'd taken some crackers or jerky along to eat. The boredom reminded his belly it was midday. A swig from the canteen and he looked at the dust boiling up.

That meant a buggy or wagon and Bixby might be coming back. Not him—Slocum had never seen the man who got out. He spoke to a rifle-bearing guard who came off the front porch of the main house. One more that Slocum had not seen before—this show of force meant they were serious.

He glanced back as Donna came under the low boughs on her hands and knees. A smile on her face, she carried a bundle of clothing.

"What for?"

"Dressed like one of their women, they won't know I don't belong there in the confusion that you plan."

He dropped back. "Someone came. Just now. You recognize them?"

She took the telescope and looked hard. "I saw him in the sheriff's office when we got you out."

"He got a name?"

"Son of a bitch."

Slocum about laughed. "He's the sheriff's main man?"

"I think so. Has he gone to check on the jacal? No, but he and the guard from the house talked."

"He coming this way?"

"Yeah, he must be going to check on the prisoners." She made an angry face.

"We might better be ready for a change in plans," Slocum said.

"That no-good bastard."

"What's he doing?" Slocum blinked to see what had upset her.

"Going in the jacal."

For the next five minutes, they held their breath and watched the open doorway, but could see nothing, except Kelly's butt as he stood in the opening, holding on to the facing. Slocum wished for a .50-caliber to give him an enema.

At last, the man came out, spoke to Kelly and left. In minutes, he was driving off in boiling dust and they knew no more.

"How will we do it?"

"Twilight, we'll sneak up. Cut the trap fences and try to get the horses out before they notice. Need to stuff the rags in the chimney next."

"There's a ladder I put right by them inside the barn."

"Good, I'll use it. You see the pigs?"

She nodded.

"You turn them loose and set the hay on fire."

"Then I'll meet you beside the jacal and we'll take out Kelly."

"Yes, but if there's two of them—her and the other prisoner—can't run or walk, we may have problems. Our horses are over a quarter mile away."

"There are some horses saddled by the corral. I guess in case."

"We'll need them," he said.

"I can handle Kelly, you bring the horses."

"He's a tough one."

"So was that one in the jail."

"They know we're after them."

She pursed her lips and moved over to him. "Kiss me for luck."

"We still have a few hours."

"Kiss me anyway."

What the hell? He kissed her. Afterward, she smiled at him, then went back on her elbows. "Damn shame we're laying in these damn sticky needles. But aye, next time we will bring a blanket."

"Next time, yes," he agreed and about laughed aloud.

Nightfall, they had cut the horse pen fence, and a few head had already stepped through the open span when they headed for the barn. Make it hard to round them up. When the guard on the roof turned his back, they hurried to the dark barn.

Slocum picked up the ladder and sacks. She nodded and said, "Pigs next."

He nodded and made his way along the barn's shadowy sides. In a hundred feet of open ground, he was beside the house. Ladder in place, he went quiet as a mouse up the rungs and eased his weight onto the roof. It gave and he hoped it was not that loud. Another step and then one more and he was beside the brick flue.

The sacks stuffed in place, he could hear the kitchen help chattering below him and tiptoed to the edge and down the ladder. Get the horses next—he paused at the edge of the house before crossing the pearl-lit yard. Then, seeing nothing, he went to the corral where the six horses were hitched. Acting as if he were on a mission, he undid the horses and started leading them to the west side of the ranch layout.

He passed the barn and was coming to the jacal when he heard a hiss. "Come on!"

He rounded the building and saw three figures in the

shadows. He recognized Donna and Amanda. The third one looked like a young cowboy.

"Fire! Fire!" someone shouted behind him.

"Who let the damn hogs out?" another yelled in the growing confusion.

"Slocum, thank God you are alive," Amanda said and put her face on his shirt for a second; then he boosted her into the saddle, his strength fast waning.

"Graham, Texas Rangers," the young man said and bounded onto his mount. Donna was on one and Slocum looked back. The problems of the fire and the loose pigs were working.

"The damn house is on fire, too!" someone else shouted in the pandemonium.

With effort, Slocum swung into the saddle. "Donna, get us out of here."

She let out a wildcat scream and, whipping her horse, headed for the dark cedars. Slocum took up the rear guard. As they drew some pistol shots, the night wrapped them in her arms and they were gone—riding the horses that they had planned to use.

After midnight, they were at the cave, and Tia, looking like the triumphant one, served them red wine, beef, vegetables and fresh-made tortillas.

Slocum guessed Troy Graham to be in his twenties, but the young man was wiry, and, despite his days of torture at Bixby's hands, was ready to call in the rest of his Ranger company.

Amanda looked very tired, but she maintained her spirit.

"We've been all split up since we left the ranch," she said. "Donna told me what happened to poor Montez. How did you get out of jail?"

"Tia and Donna came to my rescue."

"Well, what now?"

"I need to get word to the captain," Graham said. "He'll be here and we can get rid of them in a few days. Once we get Bixby and McKlein, these gunhands will fade for the border like smoke on the wind."

"I don't doubt that," Slocum said. "But they have the road guarded, and they even got me on the back roads. Let's let my plan work some. We're getting people we can trust armed. I want a bunch of these thugs put behind bars, not just run off to Mexico."

"I like that thinking. You don't want them coming back when the next guy wants to start a range war, right?" Graham said.

"Exactly. We need them brought in and jailed."

"How are we getting them?"

"Best way that I know. One at a time."

"But how long will that take?" Amanda asked.

"Faster than you think."

"Where do we start?"

"They've got a cow camp and they're busy rebranding her cattle."

"That's rustling," the Ranger said.

"Right, but we have some folks in that crew who will help us."

"Get them first?"

"Yes, that's my plan, then to take the outside sentries working for Bixby after that, and then get the bunch at the jail and use it to hold them while we get the rest."

"I'm with you, Slocum." He and Slocum shook hands.

"Let's get some sleep. Morning comes early." And he smiled at the tired Amanda. "Been a big day."

She agreed with a nod, and Tia put a blanket on her shoulder.

"I knew you would come for me," Amanda whispered when they were aside from the others.

"Had more faith than I had. But I was coming. Did he hurt you?"

She looked away down the cave and wet her lip. "Yes."

24

"How in the hell did they get in here and do all this damage?" Bixby demanded, standing in the smoke from the hay fire.

"And that Ranger is loose. No telling what he'll do next."

"Kelly said it was a woman done it all."

"A woman broke them out? What's he thinking? No damn woman, single-handed, set the hay on fire, stole our saddled horses, turned the rest out so we couldn't chase them and beside that let those damn hogs out. Did I leave anything out?"

"No, Colonel, besides the stovepipe on the house being plugged up."

"Jones! You had guards."

"I think a woman must have coaxed the guard on the front porch away and cracked him over the head when he was staring at the tits she bared for him."

"What about the one on the roof?"

"He was watching the one taking a bath in the horse tank before all this happened."

"Weren't they suspicious about all this show business?"

"I guess they were just horny."

141

"Any of these women still around?"

"No, they seemed to have vanished when hell broke loose."

"Goddammit! They were plants here."

Jones nodded. "I thought so, too."

"Get some men in the field to find them. That Ranger could be the death of us all. Shoot that Debaca bitch, too. Send word to McKlein—he better cut off any word of this getting to Austin or San Anton."

"I will."

"And Jones, one more thing."

"Yes?"

"Kill that fucking Slocum!"

25

The cattle were bawling. Calves separated from their mothers were crying. An acrid smell of smoke hung in the morning air. Crows called in the distance, and Slocum sat a bay horse in a grove of live oak, out of sight of the working crew. He watched a rider duck into the brush after a half-grown calf trying to escape. In an instant, he was jerked off his horse and three women were binding and tying him, with a gag over his mouth.

One down, ten to go. Donna waved to him and they dragged the trussed-up cowboy back under a cedar's boughs. Number two walked over to take a leak. He went around some brush and was venting his bladder when he was struck over the head with a club from behind. Quickly, several women's hands took him away into the cedars. Number two was also bound up.

Another rider chased a long-tailed heifer into a huge cedar thicket. A riata snaked out, caught him and unceremoniously put him on his butt, with two women anchoring it down, their heels dug in. Three down. They swiftly put him in wraps. Through his scope, Slocum studied the one who looked to be in charge. He sat a blue roan, wore a brown business suit and shouted a lot at the Mexican boys flanking and doing the work. His hat was flat crowned, the brim bent down front and back. A high-priced-looking one. But everything about him spelled money—must have been why Bixby made him the head man there.

Through the scope Slocum could see the man smoked expensive cigars, too, and the sunlight shone on the gold chain for a watch on his vest. Slocum wondered about his origin, since he was unfamiliar.

Out of breath, Donna joined him.

"Who is the *segundo*?" Slocum asked, dismounting to talk to her.

"They call that one Amos."

"Watch him. What now?"

"The men working the cattle—five of them are with us. There is another—has a rifle."

"I haven't seen him."

"Part Apache, they say. Call him Blanco." She shook her head in disapproval over the matter.

"We better find him before we take Amos down there."

She nodded. "We have been looking for him. I can go north and skirt the herd."

"I'll go the other way." Damn, a rifle-totting Apache might be their downfall; he would sure be what they needed to eliminate next. "Donna, don't take any chances. Shoot him if you have to."

She nodded with a hard set to her full lips and ran off the other way, disappearing in the cedars.

Slocum jerked the Winchester out of the scabbard. He kept to the bluff and moved slow from place to place, knowing the Apache could be anywhere, poised and waiting. He might have seen all their handiwork, taking out the riders. Slocum glanced at the sun. They didn't do something soon about Amos, he'd get suspicious about his men's absence.

Damned if you do or you don't. He eased his way along, looking close and checking as he moved, staying concealed, but having to make it through some open places that exposed him.

He heard the shout of someone he suspected was Amos, calling at the top of his lungs for someone. Slocum could no longer see the man, only the boiling dust above the cedar tops where the crew was working.

Then down in the valley near the creek, he caught a fleeting sight of a figure running low with a rifle in his hand. Only one thing on earth ran like that—an Apache. He had to get off this bluff and get down there. Obviously the Apache had not seen him, for he was headed for Amos.

No way to warn the women that might be between him and the roundup boss either. Slocum slid on his boot heels in the loose talus and hit the canyon floor running. His breath was short, but he measured it out. The dope business had weakened his strength and he still felt it.

He paused in some cover to regain part of his breathing. Sweat soaked his shirt and ran down his ribs. Eyes closed to shut out the biting perspiration, he mopped his face on his sleeve and tried to see what was happening through the boughs. Still too far back, he ducked out and ran for the next grove.

Where had the Apache gone?

He pushed into the dense growth for cover, and then the weight of a body on his back told him he'd found the Apache. Or the Apache had found him. Instinctively, he drove the butt of the Winchester backward into his assailant. It was enough to give him a chance to twist and see the blade miss him by inches. He forced the rifle up with both hands and smashed it into the Apache's face. The knife clattered on the barrel of the long gun and flew aside. Both confined by the branches, Slocum drove a knee into the Indian's crotch and then gave him a whack with the gun butt to his head when he went forward with a grunt from the kneeing. The Apache started down, and Slocum hit him hard on the back of the skull with the gun butt.

Close to shaking, he stood, to gain some composure. The worst was over with the Indian out cold on the ground. He needed to take Amos out next. Three women on the move with pistols in their hands came running by.

"Over here," he said and they stopped bug-eyed, not expecting him. "Tie him up. It's the Apache."

"Oh, good."

"I'll handle Amos," he said.

Moving into the open, the rifle in his hands loaded and ready, he skirted another bunch of cedars, hoping to see the man again. Then he heard a horse coming from behind and whirled around. On his roan headed for Slocum, Amos appeared with his six-gun in hand. He blasted away at Slocum, who dropped the rifle, drew his own Colt and returned fire.

Amos's horse shied to the side at the shots and saved the man. He was out of Slocum's sight in a moment. The diversion forced Slocum to circle the thicket on foot, and by the time he was around the cedars, Amos was long gone down the canyon.

"Damn," Slocum swore, holstering his pistol and heading back for his rifle.

"We have the rest of them," Tia said. A rebozo over her head, she ran across the open ground to join him.

"Anyone hurt?"

"Only the bandits and they will live."

Slocum whirled at the sound of an approching horse. Donna came charging into where his army of mostly women had begun to gather and bring in their prisoners.

"The Apache?" Donna asked, leaping off the horse and rushing over.

"We have him. Amos got away."

She wrinkled her nose and smiled, readjusting the bandoleers over her breasts. "We can get him."

"He'll tell Bixby, though, about our raid here and make him more on guard with his other operations."

"He won't know where we will strike next."

"You're right. I hope the Ranger comes back tonight with a report on the jail."

Donna smiled. "I hope so, too."

"What do we do with these prisoners?" Tia asked, looking concerned as the women brought them in.

"Take them to the cave until we can put them in the jail."

"Should we find out Bixby's plans from them?" Donna asked with her hands on her hips.

"Good idea. What about the vaqueros?" Slocum asked.

"They are with us now," Tia said.

"Let's raid Bixby's horse herd. A lighting raid and get all of them we can. Afoot they won't be much of a threat."

Donna nodded. "Take Reco and Juan." She indicated two of the vaqueros. "They will help you. I will take the women and the prisoners back to the hideout. I can get the information from them." She made a cross look that defined her determination.

"Come on," Slocum said to the two men.

They set out in a long trot; the men rode good enough ponies and they had a two-hour ride ahead of them.

"You men know the layout at the ranch?"

"Ah, *sí, señor,*" the older one, Reco, said. "We can take those horses and they will never know they are gone."

"Good, we've been lucky and not got anyone on our side hurt so far in these raids. I like that idea."

Reco's plan was to take a sack of oats from the shed and act like they were on regular duties. If no one had told that Reco was in on the ambush, he would not be suspect. So they could get the grain easy, lead the horses off to the back of the lot like a normal thing, then out of sight, cut the fence and be gone. The whole plan sounded almost too simple, but since they were willing, Slocum felt it was worth a try.

"While I am getting the grain, Juan can get the ones saddled up and ride out with them as soon as I am out of sight of the roof guard."

"This raid on his saddle horses succeeds, and Bixby might get the notion his men will soon be on foot."

Reco smiled and nodded. "He is not a good man but we had no work."

"I savvy," Slocum said.

Slocum reached the canyon behind the horse lot where he was to meet the two. He could see the repairs made to the barb wire. Very temporary stretches. The whole thing needed replacing, but it wasn't his fence and would be worse when they were through with it.

He dismounted and began taking down wire. Using the cutters from his saddlebags, he pulled staples and snapped the four spans apart, rolling strands back out of the way because he didn't want the innocent horses scratched or cut. The job complete, he put the cutters and gloves away.

"I don't know why we got to check this fence . . . Fixed it two days ago after they cut it."

Slocum muzzled his horse so he didn't nicker. He made him back into the cedars and wondered who was coming.

"I think if we get paid this week, I'm cutting out, Jesse."

"Put your hands high and no tricks," Slocum ordered, getting the drop on the two. "You should have left a week ago," he said, taking their pistols and making them dismount.

"You that Slocum guy that broke out of jail?" the older one asked.

"Yes." He bound their hands and made them sit on the ground.

"Sumbitch, you running off the horses again?" the younger one asked. "That's sure going to piss off the boss."

"Good. Let him get good and pissed." Slocum listened to see if the two vaqueros had started their plan. No sounds indicated anything. A fighting rooster crowed and then nothing but the windmill's clucking.

"Where you taking us?" the bound men asked when he herded them along.

"Jail."

"What for? We ain't done nothing."

"The raid on the ranch. Stealing her cattle. Montez's murder. That Ranger's got plenty to charge you boys with."

"Hey, we never done none of that. Let us drift out of here."

"A new judge that don't belong to Bixby and McKlein will decide that." Where were those boys?

Someone was coming in a hurry across the lot and soon came in view, followed by a couple dozen horses. Reco was smiling.

"I got them. Who are they?" He frowned at Slocum's prisoners.

"More prisoners. Where's Juan?"

Then there were rifle shots and more charging horses. Men began yelling. Slocum nodded. It was time to get the hell out of there. Juan was on his way to join them.

"Them two can ride double. Get them on a horse and let's get these horses moving."

"*Sí, señor!*" Reco practically threw the pair on one horse, gave the lead to Slocum, and they began to round up the horses. In no time they were headed down the canyon with the ponies running ahead. Slocum looked back up the brush-choked canyon. *Bixby, how do you like walking?*

26

Jones looked like a man who'd been dragged through the Texas brush. His eyes were bloodshot and his face was scratched like a wildcat had got hold of him.

"Well, what's left?" Bixby demanded.

"Not much, Colonel, they got the branding crew today. Them gunhands of ours been pulling up stakes like tumbleweeds in a big wind. Most all their bedrolls and gear are gone from over in the bunkhouse."

"What the hell did they ride?"

"Some left on foot—that's really wanting to leave."

"You saying it's time we cut and ran, too?"

Jones looked up, pained. "Maybe, sir."

"We got any horses left to ride?"

"I can get some."

"We'll need three good pack horses, too."

Jones nodded that he'd heard his request. "We ride hard, we can be over the border in forty-eight hours."

"I guess we're forced to do this, aren't we?"

"I don't know a thing else we can do."

"Get me there and I'll pay you well."

"I'll get you there—it's my ass, too."

"Now get the horses. I can be ready to go in twenty minutes."

"Yes, sir."

27

The prisoners numbered ten by dark. Graham brought in three. The Ranger and Slocum sat around a fire in the cave and discussed the day's activities. Wrapped in a blanket, and looking more rested, Amanda came to join them.

"There must be five or six men at the jail. All armed. The woman you sent with me this morning, Maria, took me to see another woman, Señora Aquiria, who takes their meals to them. She says they are very nervous and she worries they might even shoot her when she takes them food."

"What have they got in the jail worth guarding?" Slocum asked.

"I don't know. No prisoners, the señora says."

"That beats me," Slocum said. "Why stay in a jail without prisoners?"

"There must be a reason," Amanda said, adjusting the blanket over her shoulders. "What's in the office?"

"Damned if I know, I was so doped up when they had me. I can't remember much about it," Slocum said, trying to figure out what it could be.

"There is a green safe in there," Tia said.

"Maybe McKlein thinks as long as he holds it, he's safe."

The Ranger nodded. "He ain't, but he might think that."

"Where's Bixby hiding?" Slocum asked.

"Holed up in the hotel, they say."

Slocum nodded. "He sure wasn't at the ranch when we made the raid. They don't have very many horses over there. Donna sent two vaqueros with the other two and told them to hide Bixby's horses way west."

"You asked about this Amos," the Ranger said. "Filbert Amos, was the sheriff in Day County. Lost the election and went to hiring out his gun. He's a tough dog, they say."

"I'm glad he's such a piss-poor shot on horseback," Slocum said.

"I don't know anyone can sling lead on a running horse."

"Me either." Slocum turned to Amanda. "Does Bixby have anyone at your ranch?"

"He left some gunhands to guard it. They shot at one of the men who tried to go back."

"Tomorrow we'll go see if we can't take that back from them," Slocum said. "They might get tired and burn it."

"A wonder they haven't." Graham shook his head.

"Time for your supper," Tia announced and the women began to bring them food.

"Didn't you ever get any of her messages at Ranger headquarters?" Slocum asked, taking a plate.

"No, or someone would have been down here. She told me she sent several."

"They must have intercepted all of them." Amanda shook her head.

"Hey, I came as soon as Captain Rob said get up there. I got here, and right away all those deputies guarding the road made me suspicious. I knew things weren't right. When I confronted McKlein about it, his men jumped me. Then you know the rest."

"Strange they didn't shoot you."

"That would have been the kiss of death. No one ever murders a Texas Ranger and don't get run down."

"Probably right—they didn't know what to do with either of you."

"Probably," Graham agreed. "Tomorrow, ma'am, we'll get back your ranch headquarters."

"Thank you."

"We'll try," Slocum said and picked up a fresh-made flour tortilla. He glanced at the line of sullen prisoners seated and tied together against the cave's wall. They were only the start.

28

Bixby rode behind the three pack horses. He kept glancing over his shoulder to be certain they weren't followed. Feeling uncertain, he wondered what McKlein would do when he learned that he'd pulled up stakes without him. McKlein could be a vicious enemy. Still, he had Kerby Jones up front—a good man with a gun and loyal. Plus he still had over half of his treasures left, despite all the money spent on the attempt to take over the land. More than enough to do him well into his old age in Mexico.

He drew in a deep breath of the creosote-scented air. They were down in the "dead country," he called it. Twisted mesquite trees a long time lifeless made bleak reminders. Patches of shriveled-up prickly pear, seared black on the pad edges from drought. Lots of loose sand and spindly greasewood that gave the hot air the creosote perfume. The horse hooves curled up a fine dust that floured his clothing and coated his nostrils. He'd be grateful to reach the Rio Bravo and part with this worthless portion of the USA that they should have given back to the damn Messikins.

"We're about a day's ride from Grande Casa," Jones

said, taking a swallow from his canteen when they stopped to rest their horses.

"What's there?"

"Not much. Ain't the usual place most folks use to cross over into Mexico. Why we're headed there. Less chance anyone will follow us."

His mind numbed by the blistering sun, Bixby agreed with a nod. He wanted to be somewhere in the shade and have some sweet-looking *puta* fanning him. Damn, this part of Texas was a hot and miserable stretch of hell.

He mopped his face with a kerchief and dried his sweaty hatband. They couldn't get there any too fast for him. He whirled to look for the source when a shadow passed over him. It proved to be only a buzzard flying low overhead—appraising the outfit for a meal, no doubt.

At each stop, Jones took his time wiping each horse's muzzle clear with a wet rag, giving them some water and then checking over the tie on each pack. His thoroughness and demeanor impressed Bixby. They soon were on their way in a jig trot, headed southwest under the blinding sun. Bixby looking back over his shoulder with a crawly feeling in his gut about McKlein and his anger over being left. There'd simply been no time to warn him.

29

Slocum stood in the moonlight and studied Amanda's shadowy outline. Past sundown, the day's heat had begun to evaporate and the wings of the evening wind swept a coolness over his face that refreshed him.

"It must have been bad," he said to try to pry something from her about what had happened. This once sparkling individual had drawn herself up in a cocoon of silence and arm-hugging loneliness. This was not the Amanda Debaca he had known.

She nodded under the shawl. "The worst thing that could ever happen."

"Bixby did that to you?"

"Yes," she said so softly it was nearly lost in the night air. He took a place on the flat rock beside her. "Tell me. It may help you to share it."

"Oh, no . . ."

He put his arm around her shoulders to comfort her, and she shuddered under it as if even his touch was repulsive.

"Do you want me to hug you?"

"Yes, but—I can't stand it. What is wrong with me?"

"You've had a tough time. Whatever he did to you is over, Amanda."

"No, it's not over. I can still feel it. Still know what he did. Still ache."

"What did he do to you?"

"Raped me." She moved toward him as if seeking him to shelter her, her shoulder in his chest and her face on his shirt. Both of her fists at her mouth, she trembled and sobbed.

"I'm sorry. But that is over, you can't dwell on it. Life goes on. All these women, men and children, they depend on you."

"He even raped my ass . . ." She clung to him and her crying grew louder. The wetness began to soak through to his skin, and he held her shaking torso tight to protect her from the devils that tried to take her.

They sat in each other's arms for a long time. Coyotes yapped at the moon and the night insects sizzled. Words weren't necessary. The symphony of the wind in the cedar boughs lulled them through the start of what he considered her long healing process. Slocum could think of only one thing—how he would make Bixby pay for his vicious act.

"You need some sleep," she said at last.

"We're going to take the ranch back in the morning," he said in a whisper.

In the starlight, he saw the first sparkle of her old self in her tear-twinkling eyes. Her lips pursed for him, and he kissed her softly.

She patted him on the back in their tender hug. "God bless you, Slocum, for all you have done for me and the ranch people that I could never repay."

"No problem."

With a flip, she adjusted the shawl on her shoulders, and they started back for the cave. "One night I may find you in your blankets."

"Whenever you feel ready for that, I would be honored."

She drew in a deep breath and exhaled it. "Not tonight."

"Fine."

•   •   •

Morning activity of the women building cooking fires woke him. His eyes were dry and felt gritty when he pulled on his boots. His mouth was stale, and he knew only a tooth brushing with salt and soda would flush away the bad taste. The necessary ingredients and brush were all in his saddlebags beside him, save for the water he'd need to dip with his tin cup from some woman's supply. Cup in hand, he sought a source to vigorously attack the problem, and he squatted close by a woman at work making tortillas.

"Ah, Slocum, they say by dark the ranch will be taken back," the woman called Mary Rea said after she'd given him some water.

He spat the saline mouthful aside. "Yes, if all goes as planned, it will be."

She made a distasteful face. "I hope so. This cave is like living in one big casa. No walls, no privacy. *Oh, Rea, you screwed your husband last night.*" A frown furrowed her smooth forehead when she looked over at him for an answer. "My word, did they watch me?"

Slocum grinned. "I didn't watch you."

"But you heard me, I bet." She busied herself making a large flour tortilla between her palms.

"Must have been a good one," he said.

"It was." In the light from the fire she tried to hide her sly grin. "But it would have been much better in my own casa."

"Maybe we can move you back there in a day or so."

"I hope so, big hombre."

Graham joined him and they ate their breakfast of meat, salsa and beans wrapped in a fresh tortilla.

"Will they try to use the cannon I heard about to defend the ranch?" the Ranger asked.

"I think we eliminated anyone who knew a damn thing about it."

"Man, I can't wait to confront that Bixby. Where did he get his nerve to use a cannon on civilians?"

"A thing called the Civil War. I think he's still fighting it. He considered Mexicans no better than Indians or slaves."

"Whew. He do any damage with it?"

"Yeah, a few cedar trees. We took them out before they found their range."

"Guess we better get mounted and going. This guy on our side called Apache, carries that fifty-caliber Sharp's, and two more are scouting the ranch now," Graham said.

"He's a good man," Slocum said, recalling his marksmanship.

Joined by several men and armed women, they caught their horses, saddled them and in no time were headed single-file down the trail for the ranch.

"It means a lot to these people to have their homes back. Even Señora Debaca acted excited, and that's the first sign of life I saw in her since they threw her in the shed with me. Man, she must have gone through hell," Graham said.

Slocum looked ahead. "She must have."

"Fine lady. You know who killed her husband?"

"One of Bixby or McKlein's men. They were together behind all this landgrab business."

"We get this ranch back, we still have to take in the sheriff and his crew."

"I figure once we get them rounded up, they'll all be glad to talk. Then we'll learn who shot Debaca."

Graham agreed with a nod.

An hour later, they called a halt at the spring where Apache had said he would meet them. Their horses watered, they waited. Soon Slocum heard a rider coming. It was one of the younger boys from the ranch.

"Apache says come quick. They are shooting it out with Bixby's men."

They mounted up and, like a hound on the track, took

off spurring their horses through the cedars and live oak. When Amanda's two-story house came in sight, Slocum pointed to the side and back, indicating he'd go that way.

Graham nodded and took the other half for the front.

It was obvious to Slocum that most of the shooting was coming from the front gate. He saw that the low barrier across the rear gate could be jumped easily by a horse. Colt in his hand, he shouted to his followers, "After me!"

The ranch horse cleared the gate and Slocum twisted in the saddle to snap a shot at one of the men on the scaffolding. Either Slocum's or someone else's shot took the gang member out.

Hands went in the air. The crew with Slocum swarmed the place like ants. Soon the resistance was over. Bixby's men were lined up before the wall.

"Take Bixby's ranch next?" Graham asked with a smug grin.

"I guess if we don't outrun our supply line."

"You're right, we better leave a few in charge of prisoners," Graham said.

Slocum agreed. "And we better send word back to Amanda and the women in the cave that the Debaca place is secure."

"Good idea."

"There are some of our women who are spies at Bixby's ranch," Apache said. "I will ride fast and tell them that you are coming."

"Good idea," Slocum said, recalling their efforts at distracting the guards during the successful rescue of Amanda and the Ranger.

Some of the posse were left in charge of the prisoners and securing Amanda's ranch. Donna led her horse over to Slocum. "This time we take Bixby's place."

He smiled at her and nodded. "Yes, this time we take his place." He swung into the saddle and they rode out in a long lope for Bixby's.

Midday, Apache met them on the road with four women on horseback.

"Bixby ran off yesterday," Apache said. "The place was deserted. These women say when the gunmen started to leave they ran away like rats out of a burning brush pile."

"Does McKlein know about that?" Graham asked.

The woman beside the Indian shook her head. "We caught the man he send out there last night and he is a prisoner."

"Good. Sounds like we're down to arresting McKlein and his deputies," Graham said, twisting in the saddle to look at Slocum. "We ain't overrun our supply line yet, have we?"

"No, let's send the women in town first as spies. They can get an idea what defenses he has set up. Let them go in like on a shopping trip. Hide your guns. Then we can meet the women at the edge of town after dark, talk over how to take them and not ride in and get our heads blown off."

"Good idea," the Ranger agreed.

Four women volunteered to do it. They planned to leave their horses and guns at the Ortega place on the north side, then proceed on foot at various intervals. Once there, they would learn all they could about McKlein and his men and be back at the Ortega place at dark.

"Good plan," Graham said, whittling with a large knife on some red cedar.

"Should save us a lot of trouble." Slocum was squatted beside him under the umbrella of the huge live oak.

"What're you going to do after this is over?" Graham asked.

"Mosey on."

"I thought you and the señora had a thing—I mean, I didn't know."

"Amanda and I are good friends. She asked me to help her is all."

"Fine lady."

"Very fine lady. You got any intentions, you take them."

"Well . . . I will then, thanks, Slocum. Guess you got a place of your own you need to get back to?"

"Yeah, sort of."

"Hey, you've done a helluva job fighting this bunch—I can ever help you, just holler."

"I may have to do that someday."

Graham looked hard at his handiwork. "Well, be sure and do it."

"I'm going to take a siesta." Slocum rose and stretched his tall frame. "You ever need me, call."

"Sure will."

Slocum took his bedroll down to lie on. As he unlaced the strings, Donna came over, switching her divided riding skirt with a quirt that hung on her right wrist.

"They say that Bixby has gone to Mexico."

He nodded.

"You going after him when this is over?"

He nodded and began to undo the roll.

"Can I go along?"

"No family?"

"I was Montez's second wife."

"Sorry."

"He was a grand man, a good husband, but only days before he said for me not to shed any tears if something happened to him. Like he knew."

Slocum savored that notion. In the war, he'd learned how some men had that psychic knowledge to predict their death. *Today I'm gonna die.* And they did. A boy for Tennessee fought beside him for months. One day he said, "I'll die beside a white barn." He did, the next week, when an artillery round exploded on top of him.

"You may ride along."

"*Gracias.*"

30

Sweat stung his eyeballs. He could hardly believe that the cluster of mud jacals across the river was their destination. Bixby waded through the deep sandbar, half-mad and done in by the heat. He fell down on his knees, then dove forward to bury his face-on-fire in the water.

"Oh, God, I never thought we'd make it here," he blubbered when he raised up his dripping face and looked around for Jones. "I'm so dizzy and hot, I think my balls may have cooked."

"Well, we made it. Can't do nothing to us over there."

"Right. You're a good man. I knew—hell, I knew months ago you were the best man I had."

"Thanks, Colonel. What are we going to do in Mexico?"

"Find us some fancy Messikin whores and screw their asses off. How's that sound?"

"Good for starters. We buying us a place?"

"Sure—why not?"

"Good. How about a horse ranch?"

"Fine—find it and I'll buy it."

Jones smiled, and Bixby nodded that he'd heard him. "Let's go find them *putas*."

Bixby staggered back to his horse through the sand,

stuck his foot in the stirrup and with a grunt swung on. Damn, he was tired, sore and brain dead. Buy a horse ranch—yeah, that would work. Whatever so he could rest. His ass must have big callouses on it already from the long ride.

Jones found them rooms in the village's small hotel. The precious trunks were unloaded and placed in Bixby's room. Everything safely stowed, the horses were sent to the livery for the night.

Bixby gave Jones a hundred in gold to find the best women. He took a nap on top of the bed that was hollowed out. No matter. He shut his eyes and never woke until there was a knock on the door.

"Who is it?" He staggered across the floor to let them in.

"Here they are." Jones grinned big as he strode in behind the two women.

Bixby shook his head. The first *puta* through the door was short, but she had proud-looking breasts and a wonderful ass on her. He nodded and gave a head toss for Jones to go on, that she was all right.

"I'll have food sent up later?"

"Much later," Bixby said and shut the door. "What's your name?" he asked her.

"Loe Linda."

"Ah, I got something for you right here," Bixby said and tore his pants open. Soon his hand was full of his half-erected cock.

"Ah, señor, esta muy grande."

"You're going to think *muy grande*." He waded over with his pants around his ankles as she got down on her knees. He let out a sharp breath when her tongue touched it, and he stood on his toes, electrified by the pleasure. That Jones was a wonder. A real wonder.

Hours later, groggy from all the unbridled sex, champagne and rich food, Bixby sprawled on his back on the bed.

Mexico was going to be all right. Sun was setting and the blood red rays shone in the window's frame. He looked over at the small, tight ass that stuck up from the sleepy brown body lying facedown next to him. Whew, what a woman that Loe Linda was. Man, she could take a lot and knew how to do it all. His head was spinning. That sumbitch McKlein better have figured out his days were numbered up there and hit the trail for Mexico.

Funny thing, he never did know of McKlein screwing a woman. The stick-and-wattle ceiling above fascinated him as he studied it in the growing twilight. One time he offered McKlein that Messikin girl—Conchita—he said no. Anyone else would have gave their gonads to get to screw her. Bastard never lived with any woman. Had no wife. No, McKlein wasn't—he just wasn't in the mood at the time. One thing Bixby knew for certain—that lawman had better have packed his bags by this time.

He reached over and tussled Loe Linda's thick reddish mop of hair. She awoke and raised up on her arms. Her tube-like breasts with the huge pink nipples intrigued him. He reached over and began to fondle one.

"Come on, you've got to wake him up." He waved his limp shaft at her with the other hand.

She looked at him through her half-opened eyes. "Oh. Jesus."

31

Slocum stood listening to the night sounds. Somewhere an owl hooted. He was seated on his butt, with his back to the tree. Donna squatted beside him. They were far enough away from the others that they could carry on a small conversation with each other.

"You ever hear about the reported treasure that Bixby had?" Donna asked.

Slocum shook his head. "Where did it come from?"

"A few months ago, a girl named Conchita ran off with a boy from the ranch. His name was Paulo—Theresa Miguel's son. Oh, he was a handsome boy and the girls they liked him plenty, no?"

She shifted her weight to the other leg. "This Conchita was sleeping with Bixby. She had a wild reputation, but we didn't know why she slept with that one. One night when he was passed out she took a sack of gold coins from this big trunk she said was full of them and met Paulo. They rode away."

"Where did Bixby get a trunk full of gold coins?" Slocum asked.

"Conchita said he told her he stole it from the Yankees during the war."

"If he got anything of value out of the war he was slicker than the rest of us." Slocum shook his head in mild disbelief. "That must be where all this money came from to hire all these gunmen."

She nodded. "He paid his help in those coins."

"So you think he took it and went for the border?"

"*Sí.*"

"We get through here, we better ride south and find him."

She nodded in the deep shadows. "We don't have to ride too fast. He'll be there when we get there."

"You know"—he held up a finger to make his point—"you just might be right about that." They both laughed softly.

A rider came in. Slocum rose and walked over to see what had been learned. He brushed the sticks and dirt off his seat of his pants as he went.

"Her name is Toya," Donna said of the girl returning.

"There are three men in the jail. McKlein is playing poker in the Rosa Nigra Cantina and his right-hand man Sutter is there, too. I think several of his deputies have already run away," Toya reported.

"A couple of us can cover the cantina," Slocum said. "How do we get in the jail?"

"Leave that to the women," she said. With her hands on her ample hips, she did a shake for them and drew several whistles even in the dark.

"Slocum, you go with Toya and her women. I'll take the rest and arrest McKlein and Sutter," Graham said.

"I like that," Slocum said and noticed that Donna had his horse and hers ready to go. "You boys get old McKlein for me. My head still hurts from him doping me."

"Take your time," Graham said. "We won't move in for an hour yet. Then you be ready to take the jail."

"We aren't going to storm it with guns. We've got whiskey, food and good-looking women," Toya said to the

Ranger. Then she reached out and playfully pulled his hat brim down.

"However," the Ranger said, looking about, embarrassed, in the dim light as he straightened his Stetson.

Donna handed Slocum the reins to his horse and whispered, "He would be a good man for the señora."

"Yes," Slocum said and stepped into the stirrup.

The three rode at a trot to the edge of town. Then they hitched their horses behind some cattle pens and snuck around until they were in the alley. Three more joined them.

"You have everything?" Toya asked the other women.

"*Sí.*" They showed her their baskets with food and bottles.

"Good," she said and turned to Slocum. "What do you want?"

"Now I want a clear shot at the jail in case things don't work. If for any reason they go sour, then Donna and I will rush in with our guns blazing, so hit the floor. Where can I best see it from?"

"Go two buildings down and there is a narrow way between the saddlery and the old dry goods store. You can squeeze through it. From there we have been watching the jail."

"We'll be in place. Remember if it goes wrong in there, get on the floor. Good luck, ladies."

He and Donna hurried down the alley. A cur dog barked at them, but at a hiss from Slocum, he gave a yelp and left. The space was narrow enough that Slocum had to scoot sideways. He thought that whoever had put the lap siding on the last building, they must have had a short-handled hammer or they nailed it on the studs and then set up the wall. Must have done it that way, he decided as he scraped his belt buckle on the building and held his hands over his head.

Donna was cussing under her breath. He smiled because she had more sticking out than he did.

"Go back—there's a rain barrel or something out there to duck behind."

"Now you tell me—I will," she said, annoyed.

When he reached the end of the corridor, he spotted two large wooden crates stacked up on the porch of the dry goods store. He removed his hat, stepped out on the boardwalk and soon was on his knees behind them.

He frowned as he heard the guitar and someone singing, coming up the street. Donna joined him again and poked him in the ribs. "I will get that Toya. A snake could hardly get through there."

"They're coming," he said.

She bobbed her head. "I heard Juanita singing."

"A-ha! You hombres having fun in there?" one of the women asked the jailer.

Slocum could see someone doing a hat dance to the rapid beat of the guitar on the jailhouse porch. Guitar strings rung and the dancer held her skirt up high enough to make the steps inviting.

The door of the jail opened and yellow lamplight flooded out on the boardwalk.

"Quick, get in here," someone hissed, and the prancing, laughing women with their baskets on their arms went rolling through the door.

Slocum sat back on his butt and closed his eyes for a minute. This had been a long day: they'd taken the Debaca ranch back, they'd raided the empty Bixby place, and now they were going to finish up arresting McKlein and his deputies.

"Someone on horseback is coming," Donna hissed. "Could be more of his deputies. There's two horses."

On his haunches and the grip of the Colt in his fist, Slocum watched the starlight play on the blanketed rump of the Appaloosa the one man rode. In a snowy field of white, fist-size black moons dotted the animal's backside. The other man rode a solid-colored horse.

Slocum recognized the Kansas deputy Abbott Ferd, when he dismounted and went to knock on the door. The music in the jail stopped.

"Sheriff here?" Abbott asked.

"No, he's down at the cantina."

"We're deputies from Kansas. Looking for a guy named Slocum. You ever hear of him?"

"We're looking for him, too." The deputy holding the door wasn't letting the Abbott brother look in the jail.

"Where can we find him?" Abbott demanded.

"Goddamned if I know or we'd've had him."

"He still around?"

"Somewhere's I guess. Come back in the morning. Sutter can tell all about him."

"Who's he?"

"The undersheriff."

"Got a hotel around here?"

"Yeah, the Dixie, two blocks down on the right."

"Thanks."

"Sure." The jailer closed the door.

When the two rode off, Donna frowned and poked Slocum. "They want you?"

"Right," he said. "Soon as we get the jail under control, we're going to Mexico."

She reached over, caught him by the neck and kissed him as the guitar went to playing across the street. "Good."

Thirty minutes later, Toya came out the front door, looked both ways, then ran across the street.

"Those three are locked in the cells and gagged."

"Good. Go down and tell Graham. He should be ready to arrest the sheriff and his man."

"Those men"—Toya stopped and turned back—"they wanted you?"

"They ain't getting him," Donna announced. "We are leaving."

"Vaya con Dios, mi amigos," Toya said and waved as they headed for the corral and their horses. She ran off the other way to tell the Ranger that the jail was ready for his prisoners.

32

"A fine horse ranch?" Bixby said.

"Oh, *sí señor*. It has a river that runs through it all year long," Señor Valenti said. A small man smartly dressed with a pencil mustache and wavy black hair, the land agent was describing a place for sale. "There is much grass and a beautiful casa."

"I want to go see it. How much?"

"Oh, four thousand dollars."

"It better be a castle for that much money," Bixby said, annoyed at the high price.

Valenti held up his hands. "Perhaps we can, how you call it, dicker some."

"Yeah, we'll need to do that." Bixby glanced over at Jones. "What do you think?"

"Live water and grass. Sounds good to me. Let's go look."

Bixby nodded. Valenti promised to meet them in the morning with a carriage and show them the place. That made Bixby happy—gave him all day to play with his new pet Loe Linda.

When the agent left, the two men agreed that this might be what they were looking for.

173

"I'll go take me a siesta and send back your girl," Jones said.

"Do that and we'll have supper about dark."

"Cheap enough living down here," Jones said.

"Yes, but there are also little ways to make money."

"Good horses sell well on both sides of the border."

"Yes," Bixby agreed and showed his man out.

In minutes, the barefoot vixen was back and Bixby smiled. She might wear it out. Ah, and such fun trying to. He watched her shed the dress over her head. The sight of her brown nakedness took his breath away. Already he was becoming hard.

At sunup, he and Jones ate breakfast with the wrinkled-faced street woman who cooked on the sidewalk outside the hotel entrance. In the cool first light, they squatted on their boot heels to eat her scrambled eggs, pork, tomatoes and hot peppers wrapped in tortillas. The burros laden with sticks for firewood clopped past them up the stone-paved street. Bleating goats with milk-strutted bags came next. Then two mules, each with giant clay pots strapped on them, carried water from the river.

Women's shrill voices mixed with the peddlers' shouting. The sharp mesquite smoke from the old woman's cooking fire found Bixby's nostrils and he was glad when the next breeze took it away. Yes, he liked it below the border.

Both men rose and stretched. She served them more coffee in their tin cups. He paid her and nodded. This old lady would make a fine ranch cook—she had been making them tasty food for their various meals.

"Would you come to my new hacienda and cook for me there?"

"You have a jacal for me to live in?" When she smiled at him, he saw that her front teeth were gone.

"I think so, but I will know today."

"You tell me. I come cook for you."

The trip out to the ranch required a two-hour drive, and when they crossed the river, the carriage wheels splashed some water.

"Oh, it is the dry time. That is why it is so low. But see the cottonwoods—they are healthy." Valenti pointed out the gnarled old trees that lined the course.

Bixby nodded. The ranch house was low-roofed and the place, he discovered, had sat empty for some time. The sticks of furniture left were dusty, and cobwebs cloaked everything. Broken pottery was strewn on the tile floors, and a skim of dirt covered the surfaces.

"Where are the owners?"

"The old man died and his children live in Mexico City."

"How many hectares?"

"Two thousand."

"I would pay no more than that for it."

"Oh but señor—"

"Two thousand. Too much work to do here." He looked up as Jones came in the front door. "How are the corrals?"

"They need lots of work."

"My final offer."

Valenti dropped his head in defeat. "This is a hacienda and land grant."

"Get the papers drawn up or forget it."

"Sí," the man said and shook his head. "I will bring the papers in two days. It is your ranch. You will have the money?"

"Yes," Bixby said. "We'll be along." He shooed the land agent toward the buggy so he could talk to Jones in private.

"What do you think?"

Jones nodded. "Make a fine horse ranch."

"My opinion, too. Hire some men to protect the place—there are bandits down here. Then hire some to help to clean it up, and also get a wagon and team. We'll need to haul supplies and furniture up here."

"Sure," Jones said and winked at his boss. "This'll do just fine."

"Perhaps being run out of Texas was a big favor for us."

"Yeah, going smooth down here so far."

Bixby clapped him on the shoulder and headed him for the door. He would have liked to have owned all that land in the hill country—but instead he would own an empire in Mexico. Viva Mexico.

Things continued to go smoothly. Valenti brought the papers and Bixby paid him. Jones hired four pistoleros to guard the ranch. He also found two large families to clean up and then work the place. The old woman with two grandkids came to cook. Soon the tile floors shone and things were settling down. Loe Linda and her girlfriend Marie hung curtains and made the house look better.

Bixby was settling in. Jones had looked over the range and reported several cattle wearing the brand he'd bought with the place. Bixby sent him and another man to find a fat one to butcher. They cooked it over a pit and had a small fandango.

Listening to the music of the guitar and watching his Loe Linda hat dance, Bixby grinned and wondered about McKlein. Had the man escaped in time? No telling.

It was long past midnight when Bixby awoke. Someone was in his bedroom. He reached for the gun beside the bed. A strong hand closed on his wrist and stopped him. Where were the guards? Jones?

Loe Linda screamed, but they dragged her from the bed. Bixby could hear her struggling, but two strong men pinned him facedown. Nothing he could do.

"Who are you?" he asked in a quavering voice.

"You know who we are. You sumbitch, you left me to them bastards."

McKlein. Bixby's heart stopped. Those others were

raping his Loe Linda on the floor. How many of them were there?

"No. No. You don't understand—" When he tried to twist around, they reinforced their hold on him, forcing his face into the sheet.

"Yes, I do. That Ranger caught me in a card game. You never even sent word to warn us. You just ran like a goddamn rabbit."

"No. I had no chance. How did you get away?"

"No help from you. We broke out."

Bixby felt someone getting on the bed. "What are you doing?"

Fear gripped his guts. He tried to see, but the two henchmen pressed his face hard into the bed.

"I'm going to rape your asshole till you can't scream anymore."

"No!"

33

An American newspaper in his hands, Slocum set back in the chair and read the news. His gaze fell on an article on the front page: "Ex-Sheriff McKlein Escapes Jail."

He blinked as he read on.

> Both the sheriff and his undersheriff Sutter, under indictment for murder, robbery, malfeasance of office and various other crimes, escaped in the daring breakout. Two jail guards were murdered in the escape. Local officials and the Texas Rangers are offering various rewards for the pair dead or alive. These men are armed and dangerous.

Slocum set down the paper and looked across at Donna sipping coffee. "McKlein's broke out of jail."

"Where did he go?" Donna frowned at him.

"Somewhere down here in Mexico, I'd wager."

"He might be looking for his rich friend, too."

"Strange that we can't find him." Slocum folded up his paper as the bartender brought their breakfast to the table.

The man delivered the plates of eggs, pork, rice and a bowl of salsa. "Señor, there is a man over there wishes to talk to you."

Slocum looked at the man in dust-floured clothes. Did he have information for him about Bixby? He gave a head toss and the man walked over.

"Have a seat," Slocum said. "What can I do for you?"

"This man Bixby—"

Slocum picked up a corn tortilla in his hand. "You know where he is?"

"*Sí.* But he may be dead now."

"I'll pay you if you know where I can find him."

"Bixby bought a ranch on the Rio Diego."

"You know where that is?" he asked Donna and she nodded. "Go ahead," he told the man.

"Five tough gringos came one night. They strangled his *segundo* Jones to death, then they raped him."

"Jones? Bixby?"

"Raped Bixby." The man made a sick face and held his hands to his ears. "Oh, the sound of his screams were so bad. No one could stand it. My wife and children they cried."

"What did they do to him after that?"

"They took him out in the desert and left him to die out there, they said."

"Did he die?"

The man shook his head. "I don't know. I took my little ones and wife and fled those evil men."

"Can't say as I blame you." Slocum straightened his leg and drew out some coins to reward the man.

"Five men up there?" He put the money on the table for him.

"*Gracias, señor.* Ah, *sí,* five bad hombres."

"Well. Would you have some breakfast with us? What is your name?"

"Miguel."

"Bartender, bring my friend Miguel some food."

They spent the meal going over the ranch's location so that Donna knew exactly where they must travel. As he finished the last on his plate, Slocum wondered what had happened to all the gold that Bixby supposedly had. To the victor went the spoils. McKlein must have it.

"Did Bixby have some heavy trunks when he moved out there?"

The man shrugged. "I don't think so, but we moved furniture and so many things."

Slocum shared a questioning look with the woman wearing the bandoleers. What had happened to the treasure? Time would tell.

They parted with Miguel after the meal and went out in the cool morning air.

"Let's get our horses."

"Will we need any supplies?" she asked.

"We can eat some jerky. We'll stop at a store to buy some cornmeal and brown sugar and mix it ourselves."

"Fine," she agreed with a smile and clung to his left arm. "I am afraid we will catch them and I will lose you."

"Nothing in my world is forever."

"I want it to last that long." She leaned her face on his sleeve.

Late the next day, through the lenses of his brass telescope, he could see the ranch house and the activity around the place. So far he had counted four gringos about the place and a few Mexican workers. No sign of Sutter or McKlein, who he'd know on sight.

"What are they doing?" she asked, lying on her back and chewing on a long seed stem.

"Digging up the yard. Must be looking for the gold."

"Wonder what in the hell he did with it." She rolled over on her side and propped her head up with her arm.

"Guess they never asked him before they hauled him off, or he never told them."

"It sounds like what they did to him was torture."

"Nothing that he didn't deserve."

"Oh," she said, and tossed away the stem. "What do we need to do?"

"Start eliminating McKlein's men."

"They won't run easy."

Slocum narrowed his eyes. "No quarter given. They won't give us any."

"The way they did my Montez. When do we start?"

"When the moon comes up."

"Guess we better have dry jerky for supper tonight. A fire might warn them."

He agreed.

When the quarter moon began to rise, they moved in. She had shed the cartridge belts, and handgun in one fist, she held a knife in her teeth. They came through the pungent-smelling, low-growing greasewood until they were at the corrals. There, someone was busy tending to the horses. He poured whole corn from a sack into the trough. The horses squealed and stomped around, deciding who would eat where.

With Slocum's knife stuck deep in his back, the man gave a strangled groan and his knees buckled. Slocum wiped the blood off the blade on his pants and nodded to Donna. She pointed to the roof of the shed and he acknowledged seeing the sentry. A guard armed with a rifle stood silhouetted against the sky, his back to them. She took her knife by the blade and drew her arm back. The knife made a soft swishing noise like an owl on wing, until the blade's impact struck the guard and pitched him off the roof in a clatter.

Shocked by all the noise of his fall, Slocum rushed to be certain the guard wasn't simply wounded. He finished him off, taking the rifle and his pistol.

"Two for my Montez," Donna whispered.

He nodded in agreement. The guard's revolver in his waistband, he studied the house. Some light still shone in the windows, and they had the number down by two. If Miguel was right, there were four left.

Slocum moved toward the casa. When he peered in the window—there was only McKlein and Sutter sitting at a table playing cards.

"You hear something out there?" McKlein asked.

"Naw," Sutter said. "But I'll go check."

The rifle in his hand, Slocum slipped along the wall. He would have one chance to bust in the man's skull. Sutter came out the door, looked around and called out, "Stern?"

The Winchester raised high, Slocum delivered a battering-ram blow to Sutter's skull with the butt plate. Sound of the impact was loud, and a chair scraped the floor inside. Donna pointed her pistol at the opening.

When McKlein's frame filled the casing, her Colt spoke three times and the slugs hit him hard. His own handgun went off in the dirt and he staggered back inside.

She was standing over him before Slocum could get there.

McKlein held his gut and made pain-filled faces at them. It was obvious from the blood filling his hands that he wouldn't last long.

"Where's the money?" Slocum demanded.

"Sumbitch wouldn't tell us." He made a face and grasped for his side. "How'd you find us?"

"Followed our noses." Slocum wondered where the other two were. "Where's the rest of your men?"

"Sent 'em to town looking for that bitch. That whore he had might know where it is."

"What's her name?" Donna asked.

McKlein shook his head, then his eyes went blank and his body limp.

"What now?" she asked.

Slocum scrubbed his mouth with his hand. "Guess we start all over. We don't know for sure that Bixby is dead. We don't know her name and we don't know where the money is."

Donna nodded.

They rode into the village, and Slocum noticed something white draped over the back of a mule. As they came closer, he realized it was a naked body, dirty and covered in sun blisters. Slocum booted his horse around and recognized the ashen, bloated face of Bixby on the other side of the animal.

"You know this gringo?" the *policía* asked, coming out of his doorway.

Slocum shook his head. "What is his name?"

"Bis-bee. A rich Americano. He bought a ranch recently."

"Who killed him?" Slocum asked.

"I don't know, hombre. They found him yesterday. No bullet holes, but someone sure reamed out his asshole."

"He's been out in the sun for a couple of days. He's all sunburnt."

"Ah, *sí,* he was left to die, I think, too."

"Did he have any friends here? A woman?"

"A *puta,* Loe Linda Chavez."

Slocum leaned on his saddle horn, looking about at the crumbling stucco and need for repair on the buildings. "She still here?"

"No, she took the stage for Mexico City yesterday."

Slocum nodded. "She have some luggage?"

"*Sí,* two heavy trunks. Why?"

Slocum smiled at Donna then turned back to the man. "No reason. We have to be going on. Nice talking to you."

The *policía* took off his billed cap and scratched his head as they rode away down the stone-paved street.

"Where now?" she asked once they were out of the law's hearing range.

"Someplace to get a bath, a bottle or two of wine, some good food and—"

"A bed?"

He smiled at her and nodded. "Yes, my lovely pistolero, a bed, too."

Watch for

SLOCUM AND THE RUNAWAY BRIDE

313th novel in the exciting SLOCUM series from Jove

Coming in March!

Explore the exciting Old West with one of the men who made it wild!